THE SHARPSHOOTER GOLD FEVER

TOBIAS COLE

WHEELER PUBLISHING
A part of Gale, a Cengage Company

GALE
A Cengage Company

Copyright © 2019 by Tobias Cole.
The Sharpshooter #2
Wheeler Publishing, a part of Gale, a Cengage Company.

LIBRARY OF CONGRESS CIP DATA ON FILE.
CATALOGUING IN PUBLICATION FOR THIS BOOK
IS AVAILABLE FROM THE LIBRARY OF CONGRESS

ISBN-13: 978-1-4328-7072-0 (softcover alk. paper)

Published in 2020 by arrangement with HarperTorch, an imprint of HarperCollins Publishers

Printed in the United States of America
1 2 3 4 5 6 7 24 23 22 21 20

The Sharpshooter
Gold Fever

1

Montford Wilks took a sip of coffee and with his one good eye looked at me over the rim of the upturned cup. He swallowed the coffee, smacked his lips loudly, and wiped moisture off his drooping mustache.

"Jed, I don't know quite how you did it," he said. "To be truthful, I doubted you'd be able to achieve with a second novel what you did with *The Dark Stockade.* But from the portion you have allowed me to read, I believe you just may have done it. I salute you, my friend."

"Then I'll consider myself saluted, and you may considered yourself thanked."

We sat relaxed in the spacious dining room of Monty's sprawling house. His back was toward the big window, me facing him from the other side of the table and enjoying a fine view of the Mississippi River flowing in the distance. A servant had just removed our emptied plates. Fragrant smoke from Monty's cigar mingled with steam rising from our cups.

"I'd been quite concerned about this novel myself, actually," I admitted to him. "This one was a long time in coming. My editor was ready to hire killers to do me in."

"Well, I'm no creative type, not by a long stretch, so I'm impressed by anyone who can manage to write so much as a magazine story. When will you send it off for publication?"

"I'll have to work through the thing at least one more time," I replied. "But I'm taking a bit of time before I start. The story needs to season a bit before I can take an objective last look."

He sipped his coffee again and took a long drag on his expensive cigar, posturing himself like a relaxed monarch in his big mahogany chair. I drank of my own coffee and privately enjoyed watching him. Monty Wilks, despite the passing of years and accumulation of great wealth in the steamer business, would always to me be the Kentucky backwoods boy I'd first known. He was ten years my senior. As a boy I'd stood in awe of him and his woodsman's skills. In particular he had been an outstanding builder of boats, rafts, and canoes, skills that foreshadowed his destined success in river trade. He'd lost an eye in an accident with an awl while building a skiff, in fact.

Monty married some years after he left Kentucky. His wife, like Monty himself, had been the product of common stock, but possessed of an uncanny skill to imitate the speech and mannerisms of old-money blue bloods. I'd met her twice before she'd died three years past, and never would have guessed, had I not already known the truth, that she was anything but the product of a long line of southern aristocracy. Indeed she was accepted as such by most of Memphis's higher social order. She'd tried to train Monty to behave himself in like manner, and he tried, but he never quite caught on. There was always an amusing yet endearing awkwardness in his attempts to be genteel.

"Interesting thing about your book . . . that Caleb Garner character," Monty said.

"Based on a real man," I said. "From Andersonville."

Monty raised his cigar in a triumphant gesture. "Aha! I knew it had to be Joe McCade!"

"Beg pardon?"

"Joe McCade. Former Andersonville prisoner, fellow who did drawings and sketches just like Garner in your novel, lives over on McCade's Island. That's who Garner is based on . . . right?"

"The man I based Garner on was named Josephus. So he could also be known as Joe."

"What was his last name?"

"I don't know. All I ever heard was Josephus."

"It has to be the same man, Jed. Joe McCade does — or did — sketches in charcoal, good ones, very similar, from the sound of it, anyway, to what your man in the book was doing. And he's crazy in the same way your Garner character is crazy. Lastly, he was at Andersonville. Your Josephus has to be my Joe McCade."

"You're probably right. Astonishing, to stumble across his track like this."

"No more so than you coming to Memphis, of all places, to hide out and write. I thought you remained forever in the West these days."

"There was a man I needed to visit here. With winter setting in, a book to do, nothing else binding calling me anywhere just at that moment, it seemed logical to stay on and get some work done."

"I wish you'd let me know you were here on the front end of it instead of the last. I could have given you much better writing quarters than that drafty room you rented."

"Yes, and I'd have spent more time lounging in your plush chairs and eating your food and working my jaw with you than I would have writing. Sometimes I can write anywhere, and other times I have to bury myself somewhere, preferably in the most squalid and least distracting place I can find."

"The man you came to visit in Memphis . . . something to do with Andersonville?"

"Yes."

"So . . . this rumor I've heard about you is true."

"If the rumor is that I seek and meet with the kin of some I knew in Andersonville, yes, it's true."

"And you tell them the fates of their loved ones."

"Yes. I find that many know the facts already, through the government, or their own investigation. But many know very little at all. And for most there's always something I can tell them that they didn't know, and personal messages I can give them from those who died. It seems to satisfy them. And it's good for me, too. Every time I complete one of those visits it's as if another knot has untied inside me."

"Nice that you can do that."

"It took me about a decade to get into a position to do it. The writing makes it possible. Listen, did you tell me that Josephus . . . Joe McCade, lives somewhere on an island?"

"Sure does. McCade's Island, most call it. Out in the river. You can see the city from the island."

"How does he live?"

"Folks take care of him, me included. Carry him food, keep him clothed, keep a decent roof on his shack. He does pretty well, really. Did, anyway."

"Did?"

"He's gone. Nobody's seen him for months. Sad. The assumption is he's come to some bad end."

"If he'd died on the island, I'd assume his remains would be found."

"So you'd think. Even if he died in the river he'd wash up somewhere. But no sign of him. Joe McCade has vanished into thin air." Monty paused and drew on his cigar, then studied the lengthening ash a moment. "Makes a man wonder if old Joe finally found his missing key and made off with it. Maybe he's living in high style somewhere, laughing at the city of Memphis for taking care of him for years. Maybe old Joe isn't as crazy as he made out to be."

"Missing key . . ."

"Hmm? Oh, yes. Joe always claimed he knew of a hidden treasure somewhere, God only knows where. He claimed he once had a 'key' that would allow him to get at this treasure, but that he'd lost it. That's why he spent all these years living on the river. Looking for that lost key."

I slapped my hand on the table. "What a forgetful fool I am!"

Monty looked at me quizzically through a cloud of cigar smoke. "Jed, what's wrong?"

"I've just written a book with an important character based on a fellow I've remembered far too imperfectly. Monty, there's no doubt now that I've been writing about the same man you're talking about. You've sparked something back to my memory: Josephus talked about his key even while he was at Andersonville . . . he said he was determined to survive the camp because when he got out, he had a treasure waiting for him that would make him rich. And he kept that key hidden on him. I remember now. It was enclosed in a small piece of pipe that had been melted shut at both ends, a completely enclosed little container. His key was inside, he said, protected. And once we were out of prison, he was going to use it to get his treasure. I always figured he was just talking

13

crazy talk."

"He was. I'm sure there's no real treasure."

"He's lucky he didn't have it taken from him in Andersonville," I commented. "I don't know how he managed to hide it. I only saw it in his hand one time."

Monty cleared his throat and leaned forward a bit. "I can enlighten you about that. Jim Walkingstick, a late old Indian fellow who lived all his life down by the river, told me once that Joe said he protected his key while he was a prisoner by keeping it stored in a very private place, if you catch my meaning. A place that never sees the sunshine."

"Oh."

"Joe did lose his key, though. Right after he was freed. Lost it when the *Sultana* went down in flames."

"Josephus was on the *Sultana*?"

"He was."

"Obviously he survived."

"Yes. But he actually lost the key before the fire and explosion. Joe told me the story himself. There was a man on the *Sultana* who knew about the key and wanted it. On the boat Joe was carrying it in his pocket, I gather, rather than the, uh, other place. Too bad for him, because this other man got the key, threw Joe off the boat, and was waving it at him, taunting him from the deck, when the first fire broke out. When the explosions came, this fellow got the brunt of it. And listen to this, if you like a good tale: Joe actually found the thief's arm on the riverbank a day later! He knew it by the Masonic ring on the finger. But the man was gone, probably killed, and the piece of pipe with the key was gone, too."

"Amazing."

"Absolutely."

"But I don't understand something. Why wouldn't Joe go after his treasure even without his key? Locks can be opened in other ways."

"I've pondered that. I don't believe it was a literal key, Jed. I think it was perhaps a map, or description, something like that. Or more likely, it was simply a piece of enclosed pipe that an insane mind attached significance to, and there was never a treasure or key or anything else at all. Just a fantasy in poor old Joe's addled head. Whatever the truth, Joe seemed persuaded there really was something to it. He spent the last dozen years or more roaming up and down the riverbanks, looking for that lost key."

"That piece of pipe is buried deep in the bottom of the river by now."

"Yes. Any sane man would have given up years ago. But keep in mind: Joe McCade isn't a sane man. Or wasn't. I have a feeling he's gone from this world now. Poor old fool, poor old fool."

We fell silent, returning to our coffee and private thoughts. Monty's cigar went out and he laid it aside in an ashtray.

"Jed, what would you think of a little trip tomorrow?"

"Well, I was thinking of leaving tomorrow, Monty. I'm going to Colorado."

"My word, but you are a traveler, my friend! Professional reasons, or one of these Andersonville jaunts?"

"The latter."

"Could you delay leaving by a day?"

"Perhaps. What do you have in mind?"

"Let's visit McCade's Island. Just for a look around. Maybe Joe's even come back."

I considered it. Visiting McCade's last haunts could prove beneficial to my second draft. "I can do that."

"Excellent! Tomorrow morning, then."

"Tomorrow morning."

2

When our small craft was tied off safely on the bank, we paused to look back across the great river from the perspective of Mc-Cade's Island. Visible to the southeast was Memphis, the roofs of its tallest buildings reflecting the little bit of sunlight that managed to pierce a generally overcast sky. The river looked dark on this gloomy day. We listened to it as it lapped the bank of the island. Occasional sounds of river traffic and onshore commerce reached us across the distance. Back in the island itself birds called and moved among the trees.

"Magnificent lady, this old river," Monty said. "The only lady in my life these days, Jed. And I do love her. Not as much as I loved Anne, but sometimes it's close."

"This river's been good to you," I observed. "You've made your fortune on it."

"Yes, but I swear, if ever I lost it all, I'd not lose my affection for the Mississippi. I'd just move out here onto this island, maybe, and live like Joe McCade did. Imagine awakening every day in the midst of the river, here on such a beautiful place . . . maybe Joe wasn't as crazy as we think he was, eh?"

"Maybe not. But speaking of that, one question: if Josephus McCade by chance has returned, he wouldn't be the kind to take a shot at intruders, would he?"

"No, no. He knows me well. I've brought him many a cache of food, along with several boxes of cigars and even a few bottles of very good whiskey. Joe's not had it too bad out here, to tell you the truth."

"You know the way to his place, obviously."

"Come on. I'll show you."

I could have found it easily enough on my own. The path into the trees was well-worn. But I noticed there was evidence it hadn't been trodden recently — trash and leaves and so on blown across it and left undisturbed, and springtime weeds thriving all along it, uncrushed by previous pedestrians.

Moving through the scrubby forest that covered most of this river island, we rounded a turn on the path. Monty stopped

18

and pointed at a sign painted on a board and nailed to a tree.

YOU ARE COMING TO MCCADE'S. IF IN ILL WILL OR WITH EMPTY HAND TURN BACK. IF FRIENDLY BEARING FOOD OR WHISKEY COME AHEAD RIGHT ON MY DEAR FRIENDS.

I grinned. "Josephus made that sign?"

"Yes. He's got signs hung all over this island. Some with messages like this one, others just random kinds of jottings. But all of them neatly made, perfectly lettered. The man's artistic touch can't be denied."

"Even at Andersonville, I thought his work was potentially of a professional quality," I said. "Even though about all he could do was use pieces of burnt wood to sketch on scraps of lumber or the sides of tents and so on."

"He did little better here, for the most part. But at times I would have artistic supplies brought to him, real canvases and sketching pencils and such. But he always seemed to prefer the most primitive tools."

Another bend in the trail, and we encountered a makeshift art exhibition. Joe had used an old window frame, complete with glass, as a protector for a series of sketches done in charcoal on a stretched piece of tent

19

canvas. The scenes showed Memphis as it appeared from the island and were excellently done.

"Any chance he had training early in life?" I asked.

"No," Monty replied. "I asked him once. This is pure, raw talent you see. He scoffed at the notion of anyone trying to tell him how to draw."

"Imagine if he *had* been trained."

"He might have become one of the greats. Apart from the fact he was noggin-against-the-tree-trunk crazy."

"Craziness doesn't necessarily overly hamper an artist."

We advanced and reached a clearing, wherein stood a plain, small, but obviously stout clapboard cabin. A couple of small outbuildings, one a privy and the other a storage shed, were the only other structures.

"Hello the house!" shouted Monty, just in case. But both of us knew already that no one was on this island but us. A sense of great emptiness hung in the atmosphere of McCade's Island.

We walked on in and found the door ajar, leaves and dirt blown in, animal tracks dirtying the plank floor. McCade's furniture, meager and mismatched throwaways given by his volunteer caregivers from

Memphis, was scattered around the room, some of it overturned. At the back of the cabin was a small room, built onto the outside rear; in it was a makeshift kitchen — small iron stove, a few iron pots and pans, now beginning to rust, some mostly cracked crockery — and some cheap dishes and tableware. Very little sign of stored food, I noticed, and pointed it out to Monty.

"I'm sure some of it was eaten by animals, but there's little evidence of it," I said. "That has to mean that either he was almost entirely out of food when he died and disappeared — or maybe that he didn't die. Maybe he left and took what he had with him."

"Or, if he was murdered, the murderer might have helped himself to it."

"Someone who heard about McCade's treasure ravings?

"It could happen. Everybody in Memphis knows about Joe McCade and all his treasure talk. Most didn't take it seriously — why should you, after all? — but you let that kind of talk get drifting through a saloon with drunk strangers around . . . it wouldn't surprise me if somebody decided to see for themselves what they could learn from Joe about his treasure."

The thought was saddening. I'd been

intrigued by Josephus McCade back at Andersonville, but I'd not drawn close to him. Almost no one did . . . he wouldn't allow it. But he'd been intriguing, a man moved by some unseen pulse the rest of the world missed. That was the trait that had spurred me to turn a fictional version of him into a character in my new novel . . . a character admittedly filled out much by imagination. Here, in his old haunt, I began to wish I'd known the real man better.

A rough, slapped-together cabinet stood in the corner, near McCade's old cot. Monty opened it, took a step back, and said, "Have a look at this, Jed."

The shelves spilled over with McCade's artwork. Sheets of canvas, paper, pieces of wood, all of them covered by his sketching. One large piece of paper fell out as the cabinet door opened and drifted toward my boots. I knelt and picked it up. The scene depicted a Civil War skirmish, soldiers in Union garb trading shots with some ragged Rebs. I studied the art and noticed the level of detail. The more deeply I looked into the picture, the more I found.

"This is fine work," I said. "Josephus McCade could have had an outstanding career as an illustrator, perhaps even an exhibiting artist."

"Indeed," Monty said. He was shuffling through more of the artwork. "You know, this shouldn't be left here. I'm taking this back with us."

"I agree. I think you should lock it away someplace safe. We can leave a note for Mc-Cade in case he is alive and comes back here looking for it."

"Would you want some of it?"

"Maybe." I studied some of the smaller works. Most were done on stray pieces of paper. One series of sketches was done on the backs of a letter someone had written to McCade.

"I'll keep some of these smaller ones. But if McCade comes back and wants them returned, you can wire my publishers. They'll let me know, and I'll send them back."

We roamed the island awhile, looking for evidence of what might have happened to McCade. We found nothing to help us.

Gathering up his works of art, we returned to the skiff. Before disembarking, Monty stood on the bank and looked north.

"Think about what it must have been like for McCade and all those others that night in '65," he said.

"You're thinking of the *Sultana*?"

"Yes. Two thousand human beings packed

onto a craft intended to carry only a few hundred. Straining boilers, pushed beyond the limits . . . fire, then explosion. It must have been hell, Jed, purest hell! I've talked to some who were on it. One fellow told me that when the boat exploded, he had no awareness of it until he opened his eyes and discovered himself in the air, well above the river, looking down at the fire, bodies and debris flying and falling. He fell into the water and passed out again, and God only knows how he didn't drown. The next thing he remembered was clinging to a piece of floating wreckage and drifting back down the river toward Memphis. He told me of the floating corpses, the floating limbs and heads and empty pieces of clothing."

"Life's not very fair, Monty. A good number of those aboard the *Sultana* had just gotten free of the Reb prison camps, like McCade was. Trying to get home, that's all they were doing. Just trying to get home."

"Only to be killed. What a terrible irony!"

I thought about it all, then had to shake myself free of it. The overarching gray sky, the sense of emptiness and even death that seemed to overhang this little island, and my sense that the artwork we had just rescued spoke of a talented and artistic life largely allowed to go to waste . . . these things together filled me with a heavy, depressed feeling.

"Come on, Monty," I said. "Let's get away from here."

"I agree."

We loaded McCade's art into the craft and made our way back to Memphis with few words spoken. I spent the rest of the day in Monty's house, feeling somber the entire time. The next morning I departed for Colorado.

3

I gazed at the sketch in my hand and found myself ever more impressed by the skill of the late Joe McCade. This sketch in particular held meaning for me: in a few well-chosen strokes, McCade had depicted a high stockade wall, a crowd of human forms, an ominous guard tower. I knew well the real version of this Andersonville scene. This was the stockade wall as it had appeared from the area of the hell-camp where McCade had lived.

Too bad I couldn't have had such illustrations in my first novel. McCade achieved visually what I sought to achieve in words.

"You draw that, Mr. Wells?" asked an inquisitive little girl named Virginia. She sat beside me on the jolting stage as it rumbled toward the high-altitude mining town of Leadville, and had already engaged me in several conversations.

"No, this was done by a man I once

knew," I said. "I'm afraid he's dead now, as best anyone knows, anyway."

"It's a good picture. Where is that?"

"A prison camp, from back in the war. Not a happy place." I put the sketch back into a heavy protective envelope, and back into my coat pocket.

"Looks like it was crowded there."

"It was."

"Were you there, too?"

I nodded.

"I'm sorry."

"It wasn't a good place to be. There were some good people I met there, though. Too many of them never made it out."

"That's sad."

"Yes."

"Is that why you were looking at the picture? Thinking about your friends?"

"In a way. I'm coming to Leadville to meet a man and tell him about what happened to his brother in that prison camp. The brother gave me a message for him a long time ago and I'm finally getting to deliver it."

"Why'd it take so long?"

"Several reasons. The biggest one is that it has taken me years to track down where this man is."

"You're asking too many questions, Virginia," chided her father, a burly and glowering sort sitting across from me. From Virginia, who had whispered loudly enough to be heard in Illinois, I'd already learned that Ezra Birmingham was a failed merchant, widower, prospective Leadville miner, youngest living son of the former mayor of a small town in Texas. She'd confided loudly that he was possessed of only nine toes, having lost the middle toe of his right foot to an infection he picked up wading in a polluted creek when he was fifteen. They had to cut it off before it fell off, Virginia had solemnly informed me.

"Her questions don't bother me," I replied to Birmingham of the nine toes. "I enjoy talking to children."

"I'm not really that much of a child," Virginia pointed out. "I'm only four years younger than my mother was when she got married. She was sixteen."

"You're quite the thriving young lady," I said.

"What do you do for a living?" she asked me.

"Virginia!" her father bellowed, for the girl had just violated one of the fundamental codes in dominance west of the Mississippi. You simply did not ask strangers what they did for a living, where they were going, who they were . . . none of that, unless there was compelling reason.

"It's all right," I told him. "I write books," I informed her. "Novels."

Ezra Birmingham rolled his eyes, and I knew right away that he held a view of novelists I'd encountered in many others. The assumption of some was that writers, actors, and others who depended upon creativity for a living were cut from the same moral cloth as second-story men and corrupt lawyers.

Virginia held a higher view. "Really? Like books? You write books? The kind of books I might read?"

"Not so far . . . more for grown-up people."

"I'm grown up!"

"Far from it," her father muttered.

"How many have you wrote so far?" she asked me.

"Written," her father said. "It's 'written,' Virginia."

"Two. One is already in print and the other will be in the next few months."

"What's the name of the books?"

"The first one is *The Dark Stockade.* The other one doesn't have a name yet."

I glanced at Birmingham to see if the name of my first novel caused any reaction. It had sold in astonishing quantities across the nation, but its Unionist perspective on the war did not make it beloved among the more recalcitrant breed of southerner. Birmingham, however, did not react, and given his attitude toward novelists, I concluded he probably had simply never heard of the book.

"Let me name the second book for you!" she said.

"Virginia!" Birmingham exploded.

"It's all right," I said. "What would you name it?" I asked her.

She paused, frowning. "Who's it about?"

"Well, a lot of people. But there's one man in it who is like the fellow who drew the picture I was looking at. An artist."

"Then call it *The Artist.*"

"I need something with a little more power to it."

"What happens to the man in the book?"

In the draft of the novel as it now stood, what happened was that Garner, my fictional version of Josephus McCade, surprises the world by marrying well and achieving significant success in his field. But my unexpected encounter with the sad and lonely trail of the real man had me thinking of a new possible direction for the story, one that would require me to do some extensive surgery on my manuscript, but

30

which might well be worth the effort.

"I think that the artist in my story is going to become lost in his own mind, looking for something he can never find. On a quest, sort of."

"Like Arthur's knights?"

"Well . . . maybe a little."

She paused, then said, "Call it *The Lonely Quest.*"

Not too bad, really. I made a mental note. Then she said, "No, no . . . call it *The Lost Man.*"

And at that moment I had my title.

I smiled at her and nodded. "*The Lost Man* it will be."

"Really?"

"Really."

"Don't go dragging my daughter into the writing trade, sir," Birmingham said. "I have higher aspirations for her."

"And I have no doubt, sir, that she will achieve them," I said. "She is a fine young lady."

Virginia beamed. The stage rolled around a bend and into the town of Leadville.

Along the way, somebody had told me that the first experience of Leadville was inevitably unforgettable. As soon as I stepped off the stage, I believed it.

In my life I'd made one journey to New York City and several to lesser but still-large cities. None of them had been any busier than the mining community of Leadville. Every direction I looked there was a great stirring of humanity in progress, people of all kinds and dressed in many varieties of garb, doing a hundred different things, but all of them seemingly in a great hurry. I stood with my bags in hand, my rifle in its soft case and slung over my shoulder, and simply looked about, taking it in.

To my right an Oriental fellow was seated cross-legged on a boardwalk, engaged in some sort of dice-rolling game that had the attention of a gaggle of rough-looking miners who whooped and cussed with each roll of the dice. To my left a woman was weeping on the shoulder of a fellow in a dark suit; the fellow looked quite uncomfortable, eyes casting about to see how large their audience was. Romance gone sour, I figured. On a second-floor porch of a hotel that looked like it would fall apart in a strong wind, a man danced in nothing but his longjohns. There was, unfortunately, something amiss with the buttons that held up the rear flap, for one had given way and the other appeared about to do so. He flapped his arms and clucked while he did his drunken gyrations. Just below him, and apparently oblivious to him, another man held up a Bible and preached at the top of his lungs.

I didn't like the looks of the nearest hotel and set out to find another. Winding through the streets, I was assaulted by sound and smell and a town growing so fast it remained substantially unpainted, yet somehow still full of more color than any vista I'd seen in a while.

I liked Leadville. The appeal was instant and I could tell it would not be short-lived. This might be a place a writer could find worth staying for a spell.

The hotel I finally chose looked only a little more stable than the first. It was called the Swayze House and stood on a corner beside a hardware store, which in turn stood beside an attorney's office, which in turn was neighbor to a clothing shop. Only after the dress shop did one encounter a saloon. That's what made the hotel appealing: it offered a better prospect for a good night's rest than the other places, which butted right up against saloons or dance halls that probably ran all night.

I checked into my room, put my clothing and weapons into the wardrobe. I removed my rifle from its case and checked it to make sure it had suffered no damage riding atop the stage. This was the rifle I'd carried through the war, the rifle I'd used as a sharpshooter, taking the lives of more human beings than I cared to recall. I'd always keep this rifle, as well as the scope that mounted atop it, even though the only good memory associated with this rifle was the fact it had been a gift from my father.

I'd never set out to be a methodical killer, not even during wartime. Yet that had been my fate. Then had come imprisonment at Andersonville. Hell number one followed by hell number two. Maybe the second had been imposed upon me because I'd been fool enough to embrace the first.

Putting away my rifle, I left my room and walked the town. After the cramped stagecoach ride, I had tight muscles, a bruised rump, and a strong desire for fresh air.

Despite the high altitude and wilderness location, fresh air proved a little hard to come by. This town reeked of smoke from chimneys and smelters, the stench of manure from horses, mules, penned cattle, and a few pigpens. There was a reek of human waste, too, coming from the outhouses as well as places where slop jars were unceremoniously dumped. Alleyways smelled of urine and vomit, particularly those beside the saloons. About the only truly pleasant smells I encountered came from the bakeries and restaurants.

I picked one of the latter and made the pleasant discovery that the proprietor was an Englishman who specialized in meat pies. I ordered one made of pork — I hoped it was pork, anyway — along with coffee. The pie was delicious, putting me in mind of one I'd eaten in Vermont, of all places, when a prominent Union colonel had invited me to dine with him in gratitude for some "extraordinarily fine work" I'd done for him and the cause. That work, of course, had been the long-range shooting of a particular Confederate officer whose death was of strategic importance for a variety of reasons. I'd always suspected, though, that there was more to it than that, that the colonel who fed me and praised me had some personal reasons, going back to before the war, for having wanted that officer dead. The thought of that, I recall, made that pork pie sit uneasily in the pit of my stomach. It was one of the moments that ultimately gave rise to my determination to be a sharpshooter no more, no matter what it cost me. But capture and Andersonville intervened, ironically removing from me the necessity of finding my own way out of the life that had entrapped me.

When the meal was through I exited the restaurant, picking my teeth with a splinter I'd pulled from the rough wood of the homemade table. My mind turned to the mission that had brought me here.

A loud cough followed by a series of progressively louder ones caused me to turn. A grizzled fellow who looked like the last good days he'd seen had been a decade or so back was bent double. His cough was so harsh that it seemed he would retch, but he didn't. I'd later figure out that was because there was nothing in his belly to retch up.

"You all right, partner?" I asked.

He looked at my sideways, lips wet, face sweating. He breathed deeply a couple of times, then slowly rose up to stand erect. He shook his head fast, as if trying to clear it.

"Whew! Yeah, yeah, I'm fine. Just got some sort of a croup of the lungs. Ain't consumption, though. A real doctor told me that. Ain't consumption."

"That's good."

"You ain't got a flask about you, do you? A good drink would do a lot to clear my throat just now."

"Sorry."

"I figured. You don't look the flask-carrying type."

"How long have you been in Leadville, Mister . . ."

"Hinds. Estepp Hinds." He put out his hand to shake, and I had to do it out of politeness, though he'd just coughed up half his insides onto that hand.

"Jed Wells. Tell me something, sir," I said. "Do you know a man here named Lawrence Quisley?"

"Indeed I do."

"You're a lucky find for me, then. I've come here looking for him."

"And I guess you want me to take you to him."

"I'd gladly pay you."

"Tell you what, sir: I take you to Lawrence Quisley, and you give me the cost of a good meal."

"You have a deal." But there was an unspoken proviso on my part: Hinds would get from me the meal itself, not just the money. Otherwise the money would more likely go for liquid nourishment rather than the kind he really needed.

He trudged off, taking long and fast steps that were a challenge to keep up with. He dodged around pedestrians, bounded from boardwalk to boardwalk, and leaped puddles and heaps of horse manure. We veered through several streets and alleys until I had lost my way and was panting for air. But Hinds kept going at the same pace, never showing any sign of tiring.

When at last he stopped, we stood at the edge of a fenced cemetery. He turned and pointed toward a stone monument in a far corner.

"There he is," Hinds said. "Mr. Quisley has been spending all his time here for the last seven months. I'd introduce you, but he ain't talkative anymore." Hinds grinned and thrust out his hand. "Well, I've fulfilled my part of the bargain. Enough for a steak, if you please, sir."

4

Hinds initially wasn't happy with me for refusing to give him the money straight out. Given that he'd done nothing but lead me to a dead man, I didn't really believe I owed him, anyway, but I did think his little ploy had been cagey enough to earn him at least some sort of reward just for his cleverness. But not cash. That he'd just drink away.

"Well, all right, dang it," Hinds said at last. "If you insist I have to sit down and eat the meal before you, I'll sit down and eat the meal before you."

"I do insist."

"Come on, then."

"You pick the café."

Hinds grinned slyly. "That one there." He pointed to a dumpy little place with a sign on the window that said MCGRAW'S HOT FOOD.

The place stunk of grease and spoilage, and made me glad I'd already eaten so there was no expectation that I too would take part in this fare. After Andersonville, where men came to enthusiastically eat things they'd hesitate to give their own dogs in peacetime, I'd set a few standards for what I was willing to ingest.

Hinds rubbed his hands together in anticipation as we entered the place. "Ain't had a steak in three months!" he declared.

We headed for a table by the window, but hadn't even reached it before a man in a greasy apron appeared and strode with a frown toward us.

"Hinds, you just turn it around and get out of here right now!" he demanded. "You know you ain't allowed in here!"

Hinds glared at the intruder. "I'm here to eat," he said. "I got the same right to be a customer as anybody else does. And I got money. Or he does, anyway." He thumbed in my direction.

"Not when I've forbidden you to be here. You remember the last time."

"I was drunk the last time. I'm not drunk now."

"Then you should have no trouble understanding me when I tell you to turn your tail and get out of here."

"Hold on," I said. "I told Mr. Hinds I'd buy him a meal and this is the place he

40

chose. There'll be no trouble from us."

The proprietor looked at me from beneath heavy eyebrows. "The last time he was in here he attacked another customer, broke three plates, and smashed a pane of the window."

"That won't happen today. Let me buy him a steak like I told him I would. You are in business to sell food, aren't you?"

The man grunted softly, glared at Hinds again, then said, "No trouble, Hinds. Not a bit of it. If there is any, you're out on your ear."

We sat, ordered, waited. "Are you really the hellion he makes you out to be?" I asked Hinds.

"I'm a saint. He's just unreasonable."

"So you didn't do the things he said."

"Do I look like a drunkard to you?"

There was no diplomatic answer for that one, so I changed the subject. "You like living in Leadville?"

"It's fine except in the winter. Or when you're trying to cook beans. Up this high, you got to boil your beans forevermore before they'll cook."

"How'd you come here?"

"I walked."

"No, I mean, why?"

He shrugged. "Got to live somewhere.

Hey, ain't my business, but why were you looking for Quisley? He owe you money or something?"

"No. I just had some information I wanted to give him. About his family. I regret that I missed my chance. It took me a long time to track him down."

"I 'preciate you buying me food. And defending me so I can eat here."

"Just don't do anything to prove that I shouldn't have, all right? No breaking windows or anything."

"I was drunk the last time."

"You get drunk a lot?"

"Honestly, yes. It's a bad habit of mine."

"You should try to quit. It'll kill you someday if you don't. I've seen it kill a lot of others."

"I know. I know. But a man's got to die somehow, huh?"

The food eventually arrived. It was good I hadn't ordered anything but coffee. Watching Hinds eat was enough to make a man give up on ingestion. He ignored his knife and ate the tough steak by holding it in his hands and gnawing at it with inadequate, worn-down teeth, grunting in the back of his throat. He smacked his lips a lot and belched after every swallow. I could hardly even drink my coffee.

Dessert was cake topped with jam. When he was through eating at last, Hinds stood, waved somewhat triumphantly at the proprietor eyeing us from the corner, then thrust out his hand for me to shake.

Turning to the others there, he said, "Good day, one and all! I recommend the steak." He bowed to the proprietor. "I bid you a fond farewell, sir!"

Outside, Hinds grew serious for a moment. "I thank you again for being so decent to me," he said. "I guess I could have told you straight out that Quisley was dead instead of being sneakish about it so I could get a meal."

"Don't worry about it."

"Most folks don't give me any respect. I thank you again." One more handshake.

"It's nothing."

"It's a lot." He touched the brim of his battered hat. "I'll be seeing you around, Mr. Wells."

"Call me Jed."

"Good-bye." He turned and vanished into the human cauldron of Leadville, and I figured chances were good I'd never lay eyes on him again.

There was nothing to hold me in Leadville. I'd come for only one reason, now rendered meaningless by a stone in the corner of a graveyard.

But neither was there anything pressing me to go elsewhere. After a winter's isolation in drafty rooms in Memphis, my hand cramping around my pen and my eyes strained from writing, I was ready for something very different. Leadville offered it. Beans weren't the only thing that boiled endlessly in this mining town. Human society did the same, ever milling and changing and revealing just how varied and interesting a group we of the two-legged race really are.

I walked the streets of the busy town for more than an hour, taking notes, letting the creative side of my mind flow. Was there material here that could benefit the second draft of my novel, or if not that, then a third novel? Intuition said yes, and I was determined to find it.

Rounding a corner, I noticed a man I'd seen before, when Hinds and I had entered the restaurant. He was tall, with a drooping mustache, wearing a coat made of a blanket that once had been colorful but now was faded by age and dirt. He wore a tall beaver hat that had endured six or seven crushings too many and now perched like a crumbling column atop his head. He seemed to be watching me from the corner of his eye, something I noticed the first time I'd seen him.

In the town of Fairview, on my way here, someone had mentioned Leadville's reputation as a place wherein a man had to be careful for robbers prowling the streets. Footpads, folks called them.

I had a strong feeling that my watcher in the blanket coat might be just such a one. Maybe I was too obvious a newcomer. Maybe, for some reason, he thought I looked like an easy mark and someone who would have money in his pocket. Which I did.

Or maybe it was merely coincidence that I'd seen him twice, and that he was looking my direction both times I did.

To test things out, I wandered around awhile longer, then entered a saloon. I bought a beer, sipped it and found it bitter, but drank most of it anyway. Meanwhile, I pulled from my pocket a couple of the small sketches I'd taken from McCade's Island and studied them. These two were done on scraps of stray paper, one of them an old shipping notice, the other a page from a letter.

"You need to watch out, Jed."

The voice startled me. I looked up from

my sketches to see Hinds beside the table, looking very drunk but also quite solemn. "You've got some trouble on your heels. You got somebody wanting to see what's in your pockets. Slick Davy has pegged you for a swell and has been tracking you around. He's quick with a knife, he is, and you'd best not let yourself get alone in no alleys."

"Does Slick Davy wear a coat made from an old blanket?"

"That and a tall hat. You spotted him, huh?"

"I did."

"He's out there right now." Hinds nodded toward the window. Sure enough, across the street, my follower was present, lingering on a porch, leaning against the wall and smoking a pipe. He tipped his tall hat to a passing woman, then studied the front of the saloon I was in.

"What's a swell?" I asked Hinds.

"A dandy. A fellow who dresses like he's got more cents than sense."

It took me a minute to decipher the meaning of that. "So I look like a swell, do I?"

"Not to me. But word has it that Slick Davy thinks you do."

"I'm not worried about Slick Davy."

"You ought to be. I know personally of two men he knifed. Stay away from him."

"Gladly. But I seem to be having trouble making him stay away from me."

"You were good to me today, Jed. I don't forget that. I'll try to help you keep an eye out."

I appreciated that, but hoped Hinds had not resolved to become my constant companion. If so, I might not linger in Leadville for long after all.

Hinds looked down at the sketches in my hands. "Huh! I seen that same picture over in Gambletown."

"What?"

"That drawing there, the one showing the boat. There's the exact same drawing on a wall in the Horsecollar Saloon over in Gambletown."

"I doubt it was the same picture. This one was sketched by a crazy fellow who lived on an island in the Mississippi River near Memphis."

"It's the same picture, or danged close. That's the *Sultana* it shows. You know about the *Sultana,* I guess."

I looked closely at the picture, and realized that Hinds was right. I'd seen a photograph of the *Sultana* once, a picture showing it overladen with the very human beings who were on it when it burned and exploded some hours after the photograph was taken.

Sure enough, the sketch McCade had drawn showed the *Sultana* itself, even the crowds on its decks. How could I have been so unobservant as to not recognize that already?

"I believe you're right, Estepp."

"Must have been drawed by the same man. It looks like the same picture, just a lot smaller. You know how you can tell a man's writing and the way he draws a picture and so on."

"Yes." I examined the picture more closely, wondering where on the boat Josephus McCade had stood before being thrown off it.

"Except the one in Gambletown is big, covering nearly a whole saloon wall. The saloon owner is so pleased with it he's had it covered up with glass so nobody can smudge it off."

"What's the medium?"

"What?"

"What's the picture on the wall drawn with? A pencil, some kind of paint?"

"Stick of charcoal, I was told. Fellow come in, drank himself into a state, then couldn't pay. He got him some burnt wood from the fire and lit in to doing the picture on the wall, and the owner was about to stop him and throw him out when he started to notice how dang good it looked. He let him

48

finish it as his way of paying for his drinks, then had that glass put over it. Now he talks about it to everybody who comes in."

"Where is this Gambletown?" I asked.

He gave me quick directions. It was a new mining camp developing a few miles away. No strikes to match Leadville, but promising. Silver and a little bit of gold, and best of all in Hinds's estimation, three excellent saloons, the finest of which was the Horsecollar.

"I may have to visit Gambletown," I said. "I'd like to take a look at that picture."

"It's a good one. But you be careful. Watch out for Slick Davy."

Hinds headed to the bar. I went back to work on my beer but gave up after a couple of more bitter sips. Rising, I went to Hinds and slipped some money into his coat pocket as I headed for the door. "Thanks, Estepp."

"Why, you didn't have to give me nothing! Not for just a fair warning!"

"Keep it anyway. I'll see you around."

"You going out the back way?"

"Maybe. I'd like to shake off Slick Davy."

"He'll find you again. I guarantee he knows your hotel and probably how much baggage you carried into it. He's hard to shake. Once he attaches himself to a fellow, he locks on like a tick with its head buried to the neck."

"I don't think ticks have necks, Estepp."

"No, but you do, and Slick Davy would cut it as quick as most folks cut a hunk of butter."

"He may find me a harder 'swell' to deal with than what he's accustomed to. See you around, Estepp."

"Be careful."

"Always."

It went against the grain to slip out the back way. I wasn't one to run from trouble, but I also wasn't in the mood to confront a footpad. Maybe I could simply dodge Slick Davy during whatever time I was in Leadville. No reason to fight battles that could be avoided.

A woman's voice, loud and oratorical in tone, drew me out of an alleyway onto a side street. A big, colorful wagon was parked there, boxy and colorful like a Gypsy would travel in, but bigger. It had a small stage that folded down from one side and had written upon its side, THE STRAND PLAYERS THEATRICAL TROUPE. Below that: EXCELLENT DRAMATIC AND COMEDIC PRESENTATIONS. Then, below that more words about how marvelous this group of actors was, and what an extraordinary variety of programs it performed.

The woman I'd heard orating — it sounded like some sort of bad imitation Shakespeare — would weigh in at about two hundred pounds, a third of that being hair weight. Her coif was a billowing golden marvel. And it didn't appear to be a wig. Amazing.

More interesting, though, was the younger and much more delicate beauty beside her. Dressed in Elizabethan fashion, she was kneeling and clasping her hands, gazing at the sky in apparent great anguish as the big woman went on about the tragedies of life and love. Her dress, I noticed, was quite on the thin side, and she wore a tight, stocking-like garment beneath it that was roughly the color of flesh and made you look twice to see if just maybe it *was* flesh. She wailed out occasionally between the bigger woman's orations, saying "Woe!" and "Aghast I am! Aghast I am!" She would sway from side to side as she did this, causing some of her more noticeable attributes to move in ways that had the rapt attention of the gaggle of miners taking in the show.

It all ended abruptly, both women bowing to their cheering admirers. The bigger woman's hair didn't move. Notable portions of the smaller woman did. "The full performance of 'Woe and Aghast Am I!' will take place tonight on the stage of the Palace," the big woman said. "Tickets may be purchased from Lord Clancy, who stands there." She waved at a tall black man, clad in a flowing red robe and wearing a turban. He nodded like an emperor at the miners as if his ticket-selling duties were the most solemnly important task ever imposed upon a human being. "Please . . . bring no children," the woman intoned. " 'Woe and Aghast Am I!' is intended for the mature and serious patron of the performing arts."

Leadville, it seemed, was rife with these, for a line instantly formed in front of Lord Clancy's little folding table. The pretty and shapely woman stepped down from the stage and moved up and down the line of men, thanking them most sincerely for their interest. To the man they all yanked off their hats, held them to their breasts, and bobbed their heads up and down, grinning like shy schoolboys and struggling in vain to keep their eyes on her face instead of areas farther down. That diaphanous gown of hers moved on her like watercolors left out in a storm.

I glanced about, wondering if the local law might show up and rudely intrude itself into the world of the performing arts here in Leadville. It was a sure bet that it wasn't by chance that these performers had selected a side street for this little performance sample. It was also a sure bet that when the real performance was done tonight, that flesh-colored garment worn by the attractive woman wouldn't be part of the show any longer.

I moved on. Leadville was becoming more colorful by the minute.

5

The opportunity for a long afternoon nap proved too tempting to resist. I returned to the hotel and stretched out on my bed. When I opened my eyes the light came through the window at a new angle, the clock had ticked off several hours, and I was hungry.

Also groggy. A nap is one of those things better in anticipation than retrospect. I rubbed my eyes and yawned a dozen or so times, washed my face in the basin, and headed out to find a café.

Sleep had done one good thing: given my mind an opportunity to work of its own accord and generate something new. Firmly planted in my mind was the germ of an idea that might develop into something my third novel could be based on. Perhaps I was moving too quickly, not having finished the second draft of my current novel just yet. But ideas come when they will.

And they are distracting, which may account for why Slick Davy was able to get the drop on me. Passing by a shadowed alley near the place where the two actresses had given their earlier sample performance, I sensed more than saw movement. Something like a hammer blow pounded the back of my head, grazed off my hat, and knocked me to my knees with my skull throbbing.

I twisted, looked up. No wonder it had felt like a hammer. It *was* a hammer. Slick Davy, his face contorted by his effort, had already raised it a second time and was about to bring it down.

I dropped quickly, letting the descending hammer swing above me, missing by six inches or so and disbalancing Slick Davy. Taking advantage of that, I kicked him in the knee and knocked his legs out from beneath him. He collapsed at once, falling atop his hammer.

Bounding up, I kicked him in the head, sending that crumpled-up top hat flying. He rolled, tried to get up, but I was on him, kneeing him in the jaw, grabbing him by his hair and yanking his face back for a punch in the nose. Blood squirted and he yelled terribly, going weak.

He would have collapsed had I not had him by the hair. I held him up that way and kneed him in the face one more time, then put my foot against his jaw and shoved him back and down as I finally let him go. He hit the ground as a quivering heap.

"Don't ever jump a man who survived Andersonville," I advised him. "You get used to taking care of yourself in a place like that."

I picked up my hat, brushed it off, and turned toward the street. At the end of the alley a woman appeared — the attractive one from the earlier performance. Even if she hadn't shouted at me I would have seen the warning in her eyes.

"Look out!" she cried. "He's —"

I was already turning and ducking. Slick Davy's knife slashed above me, the tip imbedding in my hat and snatching it from my head again, clipping some hair. But it missed my flesh.

Grabbing the arm before he could pull it around again, I turned him, put the front of my knee into the back of his, and kicked his other foot from beneath him at the same moment. He went down hard on one knee. Pulling his arm sharply back, I forced him to drop the knife, which I shoved off behind me with the toe of my boot. "Slick Davy," I said, "you just don't seem to learn." I rammed his forehead against the brick wall beside us, once, twice, a third time, then let him collapse into merciful unconsciousness.

The woman had her hand across her chest, her lips parted and eyes wide. "Is he dead?"

"No," I said. "He's still breathing. The way he'll feel later on, he might wish I'd killed him."

"How did you know how to do that?"

"I was a soldier once. And a prisoner of war. And I grew up in the Kentucky mountains with a few cousins who liked nothing better than fighting. I learned a lot from them."

She looked at Slick Davy and nodded her agreement.

"Thank you for the warning. There might have been a different outcome without it. I shouldn't have turned my back on him."

"I'm glad you're not hurt."

"So am I. By the way, isn't your performance coming up?"

"Yes . . . I have to get ready."

"I saw your street performance earlier."

"Are you coming to the show?"

"Honestly, I hadn't planned to."

She glanced back at the parked troupe wagon. "Good," she said softly. "I'm not proud of what we do."

"A little . . . well-spiced, I take it?"

"Indecent," she said flatly. "Thank God my mother isn't alive to see it. I only do it because I have to. It's that way for all the ladies."

"You'll find something better. My name is Jed Wells, by the way. I'm at your service for your timely warning. You saved my neck."

"I'm glad you weren't hurt," she said again.

Smiling at her, I examined my pierced hat, put it back on, tipped it at her, and moved on, leaving Slick Davy looking much less slick than usual in the alleyway.

"He'll not forget this," she said after me. "I know his kind. He'll not forget."

"He'd best not forget," I replied over my shoulder. "Otherwise he'll get worse the next time."

"Please be careful, Mr. Wells."

"Certainly."

Warnings, everywhere I turned. Was it something about Leadville? Or about me?

Later on, I'd have cause to wish I'd pondered that question a little longer.

Suppertime. Another café. A meal finished off with pie and coffee, and me staring again at Josephus McCade's drawing of the *Sultana.*

What was the name of that town Hinds

had mentioned? Gambletown. And the saloon . . . the Horsecollar.

I'd go there tomorrow. See it for myself. I couldn't help but believe that Hinds was wrong and that somebody else had done whatever picture he'd seen on that saloon wall. Still, McCade was gone from his island, and he could have gone to Colorado as easily as anywhere else.

I flipped over the sketch to write down the name of Gambletown and the Horsecollar Saloon. My pencil froze over the page, though, as for the first time I bothered to actually read what was written there.

It was a page from a letter. Scrawled in blotchy ink in a very crude hand, it was quite unimpressive as penmanship goes, and even worse in spelling. Though initially I had unthinkingly assumed that it was written by McCade, a moment's thought made me realize it was far more likely written to him by somebody else, simply because it was in his possession.

I read the page. Then I read it again.

"Good Lord," I muttered to myself.

I took my final sip of coffee, put the drawing into my pocket, and headed out to find the nearest telegraph station.

I'd rented plenty of horses in my time,

traveling as I did, but seldom had I found a better one than the big black I rode to Gambletown. Acclimated to the mountains, strong and hardy, it stepped along confidently. Good saddle, too. The time and miles passed quickly.

Compared to Leadville, Gambletown offered little to distinguish itself. It did not strike me as a place likely to linger long on the American landscape, though of course that question would ultimately be decided by mineral geology. But there were some cafés, quite a few small residential cabins, two lawyers' offices, an assayer's, a general store and mining supply shop, a Catholic church made half of timber, half of canvas, and a tiny Methodist church that was all wood and even had a steeple.

The Horsecollar was easy to find. I hitched my horse in front of it and walked inside through the batwing doors. There were half a dozen miners inside, four at the bar, two playing cards at a table. A fat woman sang beside an out-of-tune piano played by a hefty boy who looked just like her. Mother and son musical team, I figured.

I spotted the drawing on the wall immediately, and my heart began to pound a little faster. Hinds was right. There was clearly no doubt at all that the sketch in my pocket and the one on the wall had been done by the same man. By Josephus Mc-Cade.

I pulled the sketch out of my pocket and stood comparing it to the one on the wall. Only minor differences. My admiration for the artistry of McCade grew. He was good on a small-scale sketch and equally good producing a much larger work.

"Help you, friend?" a bartender said. He was young and looked bored.

"I don't suppose you're the proprietor," I said.

"Nope. Just work here."

"How long have you had that sketch on the wall?"

"Ah, maybe a month, maybe two. Hell if I remember."

"The man who did it . . . still around?"

"I don't know. I don't think so. I never paid much mind to that sketch. You want a drink or not?"

"Give me a beer. Where's your boss?"

"Out of town. Back maybe tomorrow, maybe later. He wasn't sure. Buying some furniture for the place."

"You didn't meet the artist who did that?"

"Nope." He scooted a full beer mug toward me. I sipped. Not too bad . . . a little flat.

"Got a hotel here?"

"Nope. There's tents out back you can rent."

"Tents. Cots in them?"

"Yep."

I debated. I could spend the night here and hope the proprietor returned in the morning, or I could go all the way back to Leadville, then return here again later.

A long day versus a long ride. It was a hard choice. "I guess I'll rent a tent, then."

There was a folding chair beside the cot, one like a field commander might use. There was even a floor of sorts — a big raft of planks nailed together and sitting on the ground with the sides of the tent firmly attached — and a small trunk for personal possessions. The tents even had a padlock arrangement to allow a certain amount of security for the tent flap — though nothing a sharp knife couldn't overcome.

All in all, though, not too bad an arrangement. And I admired the enterprise of whoever had thought this up.

There was a larger tent nearby that served as a stable. I lodged my rented horse and secured my saddle, then went to my tent, opened the front flap to the cool but pleasant breeze, and sat down to jot some notes toward my next novel.

The afternoon passed slowly but pleasantly. My mind clicked along, ideas spilling out one upon another, and in the midst of it all I experienced a sudden burst of gratitude for the life I had been given. A new life, really, one I seldom felt I deserved. Never would I be past the guilt that had slowly overwhelmed me in my military sharpshooting days. Never would I forget the evils I had encountered in the Andersonville prison. Yet I had been privileged to come through it all, been given success, freedom, and the opportunity to do good to atone as best I could for those things I wished I'd never done.

I bowed my head and said a prayer. Thank you, God, for your mercy. Thank you for giving a new chance to an undeserving sinner. Thank you for privileging me to create stories . . . to create in a small way what you create on a scale too grand to comprehend.

I was a lonely man. No denying that. But apart from that, I was happy.

Laying aside my notes, I looked again at my limited collection of McCade sketches, and read yet another time the single page of the letter on the back side of the *Sultana* sketch.

By now Monty Wilks probably had the

telegraph I'd sent. If all moved speedily, I'd receive a reply in a day or two, and a letter sometime after that. This whole Joe Mc-Cade business was taking some unexpected twists.

I took supper in a dining hall that served stew much as a swine farmer dishes out slop. Tasteless but filling. I'd had worse . . . but probably not since Andersonville.

My stomach somewhat unsettled, I went back to the Horsecollar for another look at the McCade sketch on the wall. To my surprise, the glass over it was broken.

The same bored-looking young man was behind the bar.

"What happened to this?" I asked, waving at the broken glass.

"Huh! Some fool came in, threw a glass at it, that's what!" he declared, actually showing some spirit. "Stared at it, cussed, and threw a glass at it."

"I'll be! Did you know him?"

"Stranger. Big fellow. Dark hair in need of cutting. A beard. Looked like any miner you'd see. He must have been stove up in some way, though. He had a stiff way of moving. I think his right arm was hurt, for he never moved it at all. Done everything with his left hand."

"I wonder why he'd heave a glass at a drawing? He's got hard feelings about the *Sultana,* maybe?"

"The what?"

"*Sultana.* The boat that burned and sank in the Mississippi near Memphis at the end of the war. Killed over fifteen hundred people."

"Never heard of it."

"That's it on the wall."

"No fooling." He didn't even glance. Clearly he didn't care what it was. He wiped at the bar top with a dirty rag. "I don't think the fellow cared nothing about the boat. I think he didn't like the man who drew it."

"Why do you say that?"

"Because of what he said. 'Son of a bitch,' he says. Never heard nobody call a boat a son of a bitch."

Back in my tent, I pondered the matter. Whoever had broken that glass must have known McCade had drawn it, and clearly had something against him. So who could it be? Not McCade himself. The physical description ruled that out.

I went to sleep early as a way to bring on the next day a little more quickly. I was eager to talk to the Horsecollar proprietor, then to get back to Leadville. Monty could reply to my telegram at any time and I was eager to find out what he had to tell me.

6

It was noon before the Horsecollar's owner made it back to town, and two hours past that before I had an opportunity to talk to him. When I told him my name he recognized it. One of my readers . . . one who shared my point of view, thankfully, rather than deplored it. His name was John Gary.

We talked Andersonville for ten minutes, then my novel for another ten. When he asked me about what I would publish next, I took the opportunity to turn the conversation back to the sketch on the wall.

"I'm writing a novel that includes a fictionalized version of a man I knew in Andersonville. His name in my novel is Caleb Garner. In reality his name is Josephus McCade. He's an artist . . . and I believe he's the same man who drew that picture of the *Sultana* on your wall."

"What?" He looked at the sketch, then back at me. "That little weasel?"

"Weasel . . . you didn't much like him, I take it."

"I'm talking mostly of how he looked. Little fellow, skinny. No, I truly didn't much like him. He got belligerent with me when I asked him to pay for his drinks. I was about ready to haul him out and whip him when he grabbed up some charcoal and commenced to doing that sketch. At first I thought it was just marring up the wall out of meanness, but all at once I began to see that boat there appear, and I let him keep going. When he had that drawing finished, and it was faster than you'd guess could be done, I'd forgot all about what he owed me. I'd rather have that picture on my wall than three times what he owed me for liquor."

"It's excellent work. And there's plenty more of it. He abandoned it on an island in the Mississippi River where he lived for more than a decade. I've got a little of it; a friend back in Memphis has the rest. Look."

I showed him the sketch. He examined it, compared it to the one on the wall. "That's the same, sure enough. Same man."

"Where is he now?"

"I don't know. I ain't laid eyes on him since the night he drew the picture." He paused and looked at me with a slight frown. "Why do you want to find him?"

"Because of my book. He provided the inspiration for a character, and I'd know that character a lot better if I knew *him* better. And I want to know that he's all right. There were folks back in Memphis who took care of him, and then he simply disappeared. They believe he's dead now, and I think they've got a right to know that he's not, and why he left like he did."

"Well, I can't help you. But if he shows up again, I'll tell him you're looking for him. Meanwhile, I've got to replace that broken glass."

"Whoever broke it has something against Joe McCade, if what your bartender said is true."

"A man as belligerent as McCade was, it's no wonder. But I do like his drawing. You say that's the *Sultana*?"

"Yes. McCade was on it."

"No!"

"He survived it. Got thrown off the boat before it went up in flames."

"Dear Lord."

"Thank you for your time, Mr. Gary."

"Hold on a moment, if you would." He disappeared into his office behind the bar and came out with a copy of *The Dark Stockade* in one hand and an ink bottle and pen set in the other. "Do you mind?"

"Not at all."

I wrote a note, signed my name, then left Gambletown and headed back toward Leadville.

Nothing awaited me at the telegraph office. Disappointing. I left in a foul humor, full of impatience.

Having no telegram to read, I reread the portion of the letter McCade had used for sketch paper. It was hard to tell from what was written there, but each time I read it I felt more sure that this letter had been written to McCade from someone in the Leadville area. The letter's spelling was horrific, but there was a reference at the end to "Ledv-" . . . it broke right after the "v," with a hyphen indicating the word continued on the next page. A page I did not possess.

I hoped that Monty Wilks did. I hoped that among the stash of McCade art he'd taken back to his home, the remainder of this letter would be found. If McCade used one page of the letter as makeshift artist's paper, he probably used the others as well.

One thing was clear from the evidence of the saloon sketch alone: Josephus McCade had come to Leadville, or at least its environs, within the last month or two. He'd abandoned his island, left without saying

70

anything of it to those who had supported him, and even left behind his works of art. Something had lured him here, and I suspected strongly that it might involve the letter of which I held a fragment.

But if the letter was that important, why had he used it for sketch paper, and left it behind?

Perhaps none of these questions should have so intrigued me, but they did. My only interest in this whole affair was the fact that I was fascinated by the person of Josephus McCade, and that — rightly or wrongly — I had developed a certain proprietary attitude about all things related to Andersonville because of my writing.

There was a third reason as well. I wondered if there was even the faintest chance that his jabber about a treasure and a "key" to that treasure had a grain of truth. Could he have actually found his key and come here to claim his treasure?

I doubted it. For one thing, a small metal item flung into the air when the *Sultana* exploded would not easily be found again more than a decade later. And Leadville seemed an unlikely hiding place for a treasure that had to be fifteen or so years old and maybe much older than that.

Of course, there had been prospecting and

mining in these parts before the war. Maybe the treasure was a particular strike, a cavern with a rich vein, maybe. If so, that treasure had probably already been found and claimed by others. This part of the mountains was a much more populous place than it had been before the war, and was constantly being scoured over by eager, wealth-hungry eyes.

Whatever the facts were, I had already vowed one thing to myself: if McCade was somewhere in or around Leadville, I would find him.

I turned in my horse at the livery, but retained the rental of it. I could afford that small extravagance, and liked having a means of transport immediately available whenever I needed it.

Walking back toward my hotel, I passed the wagon belonging to the actors' troupe. It was parked in a new place now, off in a vacant lot, and a performance of an entirely new nature was going on. A uniformed Leadville policeman was hectoring the heavy woman with the billowing hair, and she was hectoring him right back. The language of both was declining in decency and ascending in volume.

The other actors were not in sight. Maybe they were huddled in the wagon. A black fellow I didn't recognize was loitering around the edge of the lot . . . wait, I did recognize him after all. It was Lord Clancy, he formerly of the turban and haughty look. Now he was dressed like anyone else and looked not at all exotic. His day off, I guess.

From what I could pick up from the loud conversation, the Leadville constabulary had gotten wind that a few things had gone on in the performance of "Woe and Aghast Am I!" that put a strain on decency. The big woman derided this, declaring that anything that had happened was fully within the bounds of classic artistry and that nothing had been seen that couldn't be seen in a typical art gallery.

Given what I'd seen in some art galleries, "Woe and Aghast Am I!" might well be quite a performance indeed.

Estepp Hinds accosted me as I neared my hotel. I turned and saw him trotting my direction.

"Hello, Estepp. How go things?"

"Been looking for you, my friend. Where have you been?"

"Away. I went to Gambletown to see that drawing on the saloon wall. You were right. It definitely was done by Josephus McCade."

"Well, you'd best forget such things as that just now. You've got bigger things to think about."

"What would those be?"

"Slick Davy wants you dead. I mean truly dead. Dead as a stone, and sooner instead of later."

"After what I did to him, I'd say he knows better than to try anything with me again."

"You'd best take this seriously, Jed. Slick Davy isn't your ordinary footpad. He's the king of the footpads in this town. He's got friends and associates and he's mean as the devil's own pet snake. He's talking about making you disappear, and how that if they ever do find you, it will be in little pieces."

"Big talk for a man who was quivering like a fresh dungheap in a hurricane last time I saw him."

"What you done to Slick Davy is making all the rounds in this town, Jed, and you've earned yourself some respect for it . . . but your prospects for a long life bouncing grandchildren on your knee have diminished. The expectation in Leadville is that you ain't long for this world. Slick Davy has killed before, and this time he won't be as easy to overcome. Once bit, twice shy. He'll be careful of you, and that'll make him all the more dangerous."

"Have you seen Slick Davy since I dealt with him?"

"I have."

"I'd doubt he's in any kind of condition to be a threat to anybody right now."

"He's tougher than you think. He's got a busted nose and a face bruised from chin to forehead and a bit of flesh scraped off his skull, but other than that he's well enough. And he's got friends who'll do what he tells them. If he wants to kill you, he can kill you."

My mind was that of a sharpshooter, so my next question came naturally: "What are the odds he'd try to shoot me from hiding?"

"Not high. That ain't his style, not when he's looking for revenge. He don't want you to just drop dead. He wants you to suffer, and to know that it's him making you suffer. He'll catch you and haul you off somewhere, and then . . . God help you if you let it get that far, Jed. I could tell you stories."

"Don't bother. He'll never get that far with me. I can defend myself."

"I wish you'd leave Leadville, Jed. It would be the best way."

"I'm not ready to leave. And I'm not prone to run from back-alley footpads."

"I told you: Slick Davy ain't no ordinary footpad."

"That he isn't. It seemed to me that he's a particularly clumsy one. He wasn't hard to deal with the first time and he'll be even easier the second."

"You're a proud and cocky soul, Jed Wells."

"I've been through a lot."

"Hang around Leadville and you'll go through some more."

"I'm trying to track down Josephus McCade. I think I'm on the verge of doing it. I'll not run off like a scared rabbit. It's not my way, Estepp."

"Listen, you may be looking for a dead man. I thunk of this yesterday: there's a McCade buried over in the graveyard, not far from that grave I showed you. Fresh grave. Your man is probably dead and gone. So there's no call for you to linger around Leadville and get yourself killed."

"You recall the first name on the grave marker?"

"No. Just McCade." He looked at me and sighed. "Well, I've give my warning, and I can see you're stubborn and won't heed it. I wish you would."

"I'll take care of myself. Don't worry about me."

I reached into my pocket to get some money for him. But he only stared at it when I held it out to him. "I can't take it, Jed. This ain't no game I'm playing. You're the only person in this town who's acted even half-friendly to me in two years, so I'm warning you as a friend. I wish you'd pay me more heed than you are. Good day."

He strode away, leaving me with the money still in my hand.

Amazing. Hinds had just walked away from money without a moment's hesitation. The man really did mean what he said.

A breeze struck me, and a chill stole down my backbone. But I don't think it was entirely from the wind.

I went to my hotel long enough to dump off the meager baggage I carried and to arm myself with a small revolver that fit neatly into a side holster under my coat. I'd wear no open weapon, both to avoid any trouble with the local law and to avoid giving the appearance that Slick Davy had me scared.

And he didn't have me scared, not really . . . but I did take the threat seriously. Slick Davy's first hello to me had been a hammer swung at my skull, and that was when I'd done him no harm at all and was nothing to him but a potential source of some pocket money, not even someone he knew or cared a bit about. I could imagine that a man that hardened could be fearsome indeed if his motivations were more personal and bitter.

Let him come, I thought bitterly. *I've not gone through what I have in life only to fret about some vile mining town footpad.*

The sky was overcast and the atmosphere in the graveyard was appropriately somber. I paused for a moment to pay my respects again at the grave of Lawrence Quisely, the man I'd come — too late — to Leadville to see, and apologized to him for my failure. Then I began walking the cemetery, looking for the grave Hinds had mentioned.

I found it quickly. SPENCER MCCADE — REST IN PEACE. Nothing more, no birth date, no date of death. This was a minimal marker, made of wood and destined to decay away almost as quickly as the grave's occupant.

What was most interesting, however, was that the grave had clearly been disturbed. Someone had dug down into it about two feet, then had abandoned the effort.

SPENCER MCCADE. Not Josephus . . . unless Josephus's first name was Spencer.

Maybe no connection. McCade was a common enough name. Or maybe this was the person who had written to Josephus from Leadville.

How could I find out? No way I could think of other than through the effort I'd already made in wiring Monty Wilks. *Hurry up, Monty,* I thought. *Wire me back again. This thing is becoming more intriguing by the day.*

I stared into the hole dug down into the grave and wondered why, and who.

"Can I help you, sir?"

I turned. A young black man wearing dirt-caked trousers and muddy boots stood nearby, eyes shifting from me to the grave and back to me again, over and over. He looked scared.

"Hello," I said. "You work in this grave-yard?"

"I'm a digger, sir. And I keep it clean of weeds and such when I ain't digging. Town pays me for it."

"That's important work. Maybe you can tell me something: why has this grave been dug into?"

He drew in a long breath and seemed uncomfortable. "Sir, I don't know. It's a mystery, and it gives me a cold shudder whenever I think of it."

"Do you know who did it?"

He didn't answer me right away. He looked from side to side as if to be sure we were alone.

"Are you a relative of the deceased, sir?"

"No. But I knew a McCade who I think is now in Leadville, and I'm wondering if this might be one of his relatives . . . or even him."

"I wouldn't know that, sir."

"What about this digging in his grave?"

"Oh, lordy." He was actually trembling.

"What is it?" I asked.

"Sir, do you believe in boogers?"

I pegged this fellow as a southerner right away. In the South the word "booger" referred to several things, among them haunting spirits, ghosts.

"I don't know. I've never made up my mind about that."

"I believe in them, sir. And I seen them a time or two. And I seen the one that dug that hole."

"A ghost dug this hole?"

"Sir, you'll laugh at me for saying it, but I'm here before God almighty to tell you that the hole in that grave was dug by the shade of the very man who's lying in that grave. I seen it myself, with my own two eyes."

I chuckled despite myself. "Wait a minute . . . the man buried in this grave climbed out of it, then tried to dig his way back in?"

"It must have been, sir. I can't tell you

nothing but what I saw."

"Which was?"

"I buried the man in that grave, sir. I seen his face as close and clear as I'm seeing yours now. I know what he looked like, clear as a bell. I buried him, just a pauper he was, and then, a week ago, I seen that man again. Kneeling on his own grave, digging with a little spade. Digging like his life depended on it. Then, when he seen me, he run off into the dark."

"It was nighttime, then."

"Yes. But he had a little lantern burning beside the grave. Cranked down low and tucked in close to the marker like he was trying to hide it, but I seen the light from my cabin yonder." He pointed to the north. "I come out to look what was going on, and he grabbed his lantern, held it up to put it out, and it was then that I seen his face, lit up. It was the same man I buried in this hole, sir. The very same man. I vow it to God!"

"That's . . . remarkable."

"Yes, sir."

"What did . . . does he look like?"

"Small fellow. Skin and bone, mostly. Not tall at all. He's a white man, sir. Brown hair as best I could tell by the lantern light, and the man I buried, his was for sure brown, for I saw him clear."

"How could a man die, then come back to dig in his own grave? And why would he do it?"

"I can't explain the ways of boogers, sir. I want nothing to do with them."

"Why haven't you refilled the hole?"

"Truth is, sir, I'm scared to do it. I figure maybe he don't want his grave all the way full. I get this notion that if I start to put the dirt back in, his corpsey hand will come up out of the ground and grab me."

"I'll bet that won't happen."

"But it could. I've dreamed it twice."

"Give me a shovel and I'll do it for you."

"Would you, sir?"

"I will."

He hurried off and returned a minute later with a shovel. I made quick work of filling the hole while he watched from a safe distance. No hands emerged from the ground; no ghostly wails drifted through the cemetery grove.

"Thank you so much, sir. I been worried about that."

"You're welcome." I handed him the shovel. "Listen, I don't know what you saw, and I'm not doubting you're telling me the truth of what you think you saw. But you can be pretty soundly assured that what you think you saw wasn't what was really happening. Dead men don't come back and scoop two-foot holes out of their own graves."

"I know that, sir. But a man can't deny what his own eyes tell him."

"Sometimes even our own eyes fool us. Thank you, my friend, for talking to me today. And if you should ever see anybody poking around this grave again, would you let me know? I'm staying in the Swayze. Jed Wells."

"I'll do it, Mr. Wells. My name is Baudy. Baudy Wash."

"Watch out for the boogers and ghosts, Baudy."

"You do the same, sir."

7

I was all the more eager to get Monty's telegram now. What I'd learned from Baudy Wash had sparked an interesting theory in my mind. I had a good notion of who the grave-digging "booger" might have been . . . but the why was still an unanswered question.

Back at the hotel I found a sealed envelope stuck between the door frame and the door into my room. The telegram had arrived! But it wasn't the case. This was an unmarked, violet-colored envelope, no bigger than the palm of my hand and sealed with a blob of wax.

Inside my room, I opened the envelope and read the brief letter inside it, written in a delicate hand on stationery that matched the envelope.

"Mr. Wells," it said, "I write to you seeking your help, not on behalf of myself but of another. We met, you and I, in the alleyway when you so effectively put off the thief who attacked you. My name is Margaret Rains and I am the actress with whom you conversed. Having learned your name when we met, I was surprised to hear it mentioned again by another actress of our troupe, but in a manner making reference to a time many years ago and circumstances utterly different from the present. In any case, I have revealed your presence here to my fellow actress, and she wishes to see you and perhaps seek your aid in a troubling situation that has imposed itself upon her.

"Forgive my intrusion if it is in any manner ill-advised or undesirable. I seek only the welfare of my dear friend, who I believe to be in authentic danger from a man of ill will and violent disposition who has in a deranged manner attached himself to her. Her name is Katrina Ashe, and you will, I trust, recall her clearly. I implore you, if you are inclined charitably toward the sister of a woman you would have married, to come to our wagon this day and speak to Katrina. She is aware of your presence in this town and would be touched and comforted by your visit. How much she will tell you of her circumstance beyond what I have already written, I shall leave to her. I remain cordially yours, Margaret Rains."

Katrina Ashe! A name from the past . . . a past I sometimes could hardly remember. A time before war and sharpshooting and the hell of Andersonville. A time I would gladly return to again, if such were possible.

The last time I'd seen Katrina Ashe, she had been a scruffy-headed little freckle-face who dressed and acted more like a rowdy boy than the little girl she was. She'd been in many ways the opposite of her older sister, Kathleen . . . a young woman I had fully intended to marry.

Kathleen . . . gone from me forever. To this day I cursed the fever that had taken her life. I had never felt toward another woman since the depth of feeling that Kathleen Ashe had roused in me.

Now her sister was here . . . and part of a traveling band of performers who tended to get into trouble with the local law for the nature of their shows. Good thing in a way that Kathleen wasn't around to see it.

I lingered in my room only a few minutes, lying down and propping up my feet for a very brief rest. Then I was up, washing my face and hair, neatening my clothing. And off to see what the years had made of Katrina Ashe, the boyish little scrapper I remembered from Kentucky.

■ ■ ■ ■

The wagon was parked in yet another empty lot. No movement around it. It actually looked abandoned.

I rapped on its side. "Hello!"

It was evident no one was inside. I walked around the wagon, puzzled, wondering where to find the troupe. Perhaps they were at the show hall, rehearsing.

As I rounded the end of the wagon, I saw a black man approaching. For a moment I thought it was Baudy from the graveyard. Instead it proved to be Lord Clancy, still in his "civilian" garb.

"May I help you, sir?" he said.

"I'm looking for Margaret Rains or Katrina Ashe," I said.

"I'm obliged to ask you why, sir. Part of my job is to protect these young women. No offense intended."

"I take none. I can see that they might need defending in the line of work they are in." I held up the letter from Margaret Rains. "I received this from Miss Rains, asking me to come to see Miss Ashe, with whom I was once acquainted."

He eyed the envelope and evidently recognized its type as what Margaret Rains used.

He nodded. "I wish I could help you, sir, but all the others are engaged elsewhere just now."

"The show hall?"

"The jail, I regret to say."

"Ah."

"There is little appreciation for the freedom of artists to express themselves."

"As in revealing much of themselves to the public eye?"

"Baring their souls, sir."

"I doubt it was their souls they were jailed for baring."

Lord Clancy was beginning to look offended. "I shall tell the ladies that you came calling," he said.

"Perhaps I can call on them at the jail."

He gave me a look that told me this might not be a good idea. And as I reconsidered it, I realized he was right. I doubted that the younger sister of my long-lost fiancée would relish greeting me while she was jailed for participation in an indecent performance.

"When will they be freed?" I asked.

"I don't know, sir. They sometimes make a point of staying jailed for a time. It draws attention . . . makes sure of big crowds the next town up the road."

"I see. Well, I'll come around again later.

If you would, please do leave word with Miss Rains that I received her letter and did come."

"I'll do that, Mister . . ."

"Jedediah Wells."

I saw him . . . I was nearly sure. It had been many a year since I'd laid eyes on Josephus McCade, but the man I'd just glimpsed surely did look like him. Still almost as spare of frame as he'd been in the starvation days of Andersonville.

The glimpse was up an alleyway. I passed it, glanced to the left, and on the street beyond saw McCade, walking in the opposite direction I was. The sighting was no more than two seconds in duration, if that, but still I was sure of what I'd seen.

I cut through the alley on a run and entered the street. No sign of him! How could he have vanished so quickly?

There was a saloon on the left side of the street, close enough that maybe he'd gone in there. I checked and found it full, but there was no sign of McCade.

But there was a rear door, standing open. He could have walked out that way. I worked my way through the crowd and went out the back way myself. No McCade. I shook my head. Shouldn't have taken the time to come this way. Wherever he was, he'd probably turned enough corners by now to make it hopeless for me to locate him. He'd always been a spry, fast type, even in the crowded prison camp.

I turned right and went back to the street I'd left, then across it and into a broad alley. At the end I turned right, then left again, and found myself among shacks and sheds, a residential area in the poorer part of town. I was searching randomly now, without much hope of finding him. But it was encouraging to have spotted him. If I saw him once by chance I could see him again in like manner.

For thirty minutes I moved about in this haphazard fashion, hoping for another lucky glimpse. But luck was not on my side.

In the course of my moving about, the skies had clouded over. Thunder rumbled on the horizon. I walked to the end of the alleyway I was in and studied the sky. The magnificent mountains, the vast, roiling sky, filled me with awe. What a grand place this was!

I studied the sky for several minutes, then decided to give up for the moment on finding McCade. Time to return to the hotel before the rain set in.

I turned to go, and as I did so, something

heavy crashed atop my head. I twisted as I fell, my eyes catching only the briefest glimpse of the bruised but grinning face of Slick Davy as I went down. Then there was nothing but blackness and numbness, followed at once by no awareness at all.

I awakened in pain, weak and limp yet still standing. My wrists hurt, as did my neck. My eyes didn't want to open, and refused for a full minute to focus themselves when at last they did open.

A face looked back at me. Pallid, broad, possessed of eyes that were like windows opened wide to reveal a deep lack of intelligence. The brown orbs gazed at me, then receded.

"He's awake, Davy, he's awake!"

The ugly, bruised, swollen face of Slick Davy the footpad now appeared before me. He glared into my eyes and grinned slowly.

"Thought it was done, didn't you! Thought you'd had the best of old Slick! Now it's your turn, damn your eyes! Now it's Slick Davy's time to have some fun!"

I turned my head, painfully, and looked around. I was in a cellar, wrists tied tightly with coarse ropes. My feet were two inches from the floor; when I stretched them I was able to barely touch the ground, but lacked the ability to give myself any real support.

I looked up and saw that the rope binding my wrists together was hung over a spike driven into the heavy wooden support pole at my back. I was literally strung up. My feet were bound together, but not tied to the post, I suppose because tying them to the post would have given me a little bit of additional support and made this situation less painful.

And foggy-headed though I was, I had already figured out that the point of all this was pain.

Slick Davy's grinning visage moved within a foot of my face. His breath was as foul as his looks. Something glittering flashed an inch from my nose.

"Going to cut you," Davy said. "I'm going to slice you up like a potato for frying."

The other man with him came into view just behind him. He looked quite frightened. "Davy, you going to kill him?"

"Not fast," Davy said. "Very slow."

"Davy, don't do that. I don't want to be part of no murder."

"Shut your mouth, Calvert. And keep it shut. You're already deep into this and there's no backing out now."

"I don't want to be part of no murder!"

"Nobody will know who did it, Calvert.

Nobody will be able to prove it."

I looked around, searching for . . . I don't know. Anything that might be helpful. I tried to slide my ropes forward on the spike, to move them off, but my weight worked against me. My arms, already stretched and strained even before I'd regained consciousness, were weak and unresponsive, full of pain.

Light glimmered above me. I twisted my eyes in their sockets as far as I could. An opening through the cellar wall, light streaming in . . . a ventilation hole. A shadow moved across the light, then another in the opposite direction. People walking . . . I was looking up to the street.

If I yelled loudly enough . . .

Calvert was shaking his head when I looked forward again. He had Slick Davy's attention for the moment.

"Davy, you can't kill nobody here. People will know you did it."

"Not if you don't talk, they won't."

"Somebody followed us, Davy."

"The hell!"

"It's the truth . . . I didn't want to tell you. But somebody followed."

"You're lying. You're trying to keep me from killing him. Damn it, I knew I shouldn't have counted on you!"

"We were followed, Davy. The same man you robbed this morning. He seen us, Davy. He followed. He seen us with this one here. You can't kill this man, because the one following will know we did it. He'll tell."

Slick Davy cussed. I hung there trying to maintain consciousness and figure out whether Calvert was telling the truth or for some reason trying to save my skin. Either way, I was behind him. *Keep talking, Calvert. Buy me time.*

For what, though? What could I do?

Another shadow passed the opening. I wanted to shout, scream out at the top of my lungs. But I knew that as soon as I did that, one of two things would happen: Slick Davy would panic and run, or Slick Davy would cut my throat on the spot. And either way, my shout very well might go ignored. In Leadville there were plenty of drunks, plenty of footpads . . . plenty of yells and screams even when things were normal.

But it was terribly frustrating to be so close to daylight and the normal flow of humanity, yet unable to do a blasted thing about it without getting myself killed.

"I ain't lying to you, Davy," Calvert said. "I should have told you sooner. I know I should have. But I didn't know you were going to kill nobody."

"What the hell did you think I was going to do, then? Present him an award for knowing the most Bible verses? That bastard nearly beat me to death . . . you think Slick Davy lets that go unanswered?"

"I won't be part of no murder, Davy."

"Then be the victim of one." With that he drove his knife into the chest of Calvert, who shuddered, fell to his knees, and remained in that posture. A tilt of Davy's hand, and Calvert fell backward, his feet resting under his thighs.

Davy turned to me and smiled. "Your turn now. But much slower."

He advanced. When he was close, I kicked my bound feet out together and caught him in the belly. He stumbled backward and fell on his rump. There he sat a moment, disbelieving, then got up with a roar and ran at me. This time my kick got him in the chest, though the effort of it felt it would tear my arms from their sockets.

I'd saved myself twice from a cutting, but I'd only made him more angry. And this time he advanced from the side, where I couldn't kick nearly so effectively.

Bracing myself, I said what I believed would be my final prayer, and sought to stir my fortitude so that I would die well and bravely . . .

Calvert rose. Like a phoenix, or a phantom. He groaned and grunted. Slick Davy wheeled, facing him.

With effort I kicked my feet out to the side and sent Slick Davy staggering toward the cellar door.

It burst open just as he reached it, and a burly, dark-haired, bearded man came through, bowie knife in hand.

"You!" he bellowed at Slick Davy. "Think you can rob me, do you?"

He slashed at the footpad and cut a swath across his face. Slick Davy screamed like a scared girl.

"Did you think I'd not find you?" he said. "You think I'd just roll over?"

He slashed again. Another gash, this one across the other cheek.

I put my feet back against the post and pushed up and out. With an exertion I managed to scoot the ropes that bound my wrist a little farther forward, nearer the end of the spike.

Calvert, making blubbering noises, staggering, bleeding, had pulled a knife from somewhere on his person. He stuck it into Slick Davy's shoulder.

I pushed again, scooted my ropes forward another inch.

Slick Davy, beset from two sides, spun and

stabbed Calvert three times, twice in the chest, once in the neck.

Calvert staggered back, went down again, and this time did not rise.

The newcomer slashed again at Davy, but he dodged the blow. I continued to struggle, working my way closer and closer to the edge of the spike. With luck I could push off it entirely, and this welcome new intruder would keep Davy too busy to stop me.

Cursing, roaring, slashing, the two of them went at it. Busy as I was, I noticed something odd about the man fighting with Davy. He moved stiffly, the knife in his left hand and his right arm seemingly dead.

Slick Davy stabbed suddenly, burying his knife deeply into the right arm of his attacker. The man stepped backward, but did not flinch, even though the blade had buried itself nearly to the hilt in his arm. It remained there, pulled free of Davy's hand as the man stepped back.

He looked down at the knife in his arm, laughed, advanced toward Davy.

I made it forward two more inches. Nearly to the end of the spike now . . .

Davy made a desperate lunge to retrieve his knife from the arm of his opponent. But he missed, grabbing the arm instead. He pulled back . . .

The arm came off, pulling right out of the sleeve. Slick Davy's eyes bulged in surprise and he dropped the arm reflexively.

The arm's owner laughed again. Glanced my way . . . and threw his knife. It sailed through the air and thunked into the wood post just above my head and between my arms. The shock of it made me move, and my wrists slid back on the spike again, all the way to the post. I was now no better off than when I'd started.

His hand now emptied, the one-armed man reached down and picked up his missing limb, which as best I could tell was made of oak. It moved stiffly at the elbow, as if on a hinge. The one-armed man gave it a kind of pop, and it locked in place. Slick Davy's knife remained imbedded in the arm.

He swung it suddenly and struck Slick Davy hard on the side of the head. Davy went down with a horrible grunt. The man raised the arm and hit Davy with it again, then again and again. Davy made terrible noises, tried to get away, but his opponent was relentless, heartless. He beat the footpad with the arm, using it as a club. Davy tried again and again to rise, but each time the swinging arm drove him down. The sounds both of Davy's pleas and the blows themselves became harder and harder to hear.

I began struggling again to get off the spike, but my progress was slow. Meanwhile, a man was being beaten to death right before me . . . and so horrific was the beating that I found myself actually feeling sorry for a man who had been prepared to carve me like a roasted hen until I died.

At last it was over. Slick Davy, now a broken piece of formerly human pulp, lay unbreathing on the cellar floor. His killer stood over him, holding that hinged arm of carved wood, his shoulders stooped, back heaving with each breath.

He laughed softly, and said something to the dead man that I could not make out. Then he turned slowly to face me.

"What was he going to do to you?" he asked me.

"Things I'm glad did not happen," I said. My voice was a rasp. "Help me down, would you?"

He said nothing. Instead he stripped off his shirt and began working that artificial arm back into place. It fit on his thick body with some sort of combination of straps and belts.

"Some help, sir?" I asked.

When he had his false arm properly on

again, he put on his shirt. He advanced and stood before me, then reached up and pulled his bowie out of the post. He wiped it on his trousers.

"Can't help you, friend," he said. "I think you've seen a little too much here tonight."

My heart sank. I prepared to kick him away just as I had Slick Davy. But he was too clever. He kicked up a foot and pressed my bound ankles back against the post.

"Don't worry," he said. "I won't make you suffer."

He drew back his fist. I watched it fly toward my face with the apparent speed of a bullet. Then a terrible, jolting thud, a burst of pain, and nothing.

8

"Well, you're with us again. Good."

I tried to focus my eyes and found it difficult. Blinking a few times, I finally succeeded well enough to make out a broad, ruddy face looking down at me. Hair once red, now mostly a dirty white, framed the face. The eyes looked tired and strained.

"Where am I?"

"I'm a physician. Patrick McSween," he said. "There's been some worry that you might not rejoin us in the living world. 'Exaggerated,' I told them. 'Exaggerated. He's taken a bruising, but he'll be fine.' And I was right. Your ordeal is through, young man."

I'd quit thinking of myself as young nearly ten years ago, and I surely didn't feel young now. And at the moment I couldn't remember what ordeal I'd been through. I could hardly remember my own name.

"What happened?"

"That's the question the local marshal will be putting to you. Finding a man hung to a post, beaten nearly to death, with two other corpses on the floor nearby him, raises a few questions."

That brought it all back. I groaned and closed my eyes. The horror of it all overwhelmed me, went through me like a great shudder.

The doctor must have detected a change in my appearance, because he moved to examine me quickly, taking my pulse, laying a hand across my brow.

"How bad hurt am I?" I asked him.

"Not nearly as bad hurt as you'd have been had not the policeman arrived when he did. Apparently the man beating you had gotten in only a few blows before the policeman's arrival drove him off."

Old One-arm. I remembered him in vivid detail and would be glad to share my recollections with the marshal. "Did the man get away?"

"I believe he did, sir. There were two ways out of that cellar. The deputy came in one, he went out the other."

"I want to talk to the marshal."

"I'll fetch him."

Marshal Martin Duggan was a squarely

102

built fellow with blue eyes and a voice that bore the inflections of his native Ireland and his childhood home of New York City. I'd already heard this man's reputation as a fearless enforcer of the law who dealt with the local roughs on their own level. He'd come into office on the heels of two less-successful marshals. The first had left under threat of his life, the second had been murdered. Duggan had a job few would envy.

He sat in a straight-backed chair in the doctor's office and interviewed me as I slowly and gingerly dressed myself. Every movement hurt. My arm sockets ached, having been terribly strained when I hung by the wrists from that spike. And the painful rope burns around my wrists would linger for many days, I anticipated.

"So, here's where we stand, Mr. Wells," he said. "My officer hears a suspicious amount of yelling from out of a cellar, makes his way in, and sees a bear of a man going out the other way. On the post hangs you, limp as a dishrag, and on the floor are Slick Davy, beaten into a state resembling that of mashed potatoes, and Calvert Smith, another local footpad and associate of Slick Davy. Seems to me there's a story waiting to be told here."

"It's a simple one, really," I said. "I was warned shortly after I reached Leadville that Slick Davy had spotted me and thought me a swell and an easy mark. He tried to rob me and found I was neither. I left him beaten in an alley. There's a witness to it all, should you need her. An actress with that traveling troupe in town now."

"Ah, yes. We've met, that gaggle and I. Go on."

"Anyway, Slick Davy didn't like being beaten and apparently decided to do me one better. He knocked me cold in an alley, and when I came to I was tied to that post and he was ready to carve me up. Calvert had helped him get me there but got frightened and declared he didn't want to be part of a murder. That made Slick Davy mad and he killed him on the spot. Then, when he was ready to come deal with me, this one-armed fellow came in and Davy had a new problem to occupy him."

"Wait . . . one-armed, you say? My officer said nothing of that."

"Because the man has an artificial arm. Wooden, hinged at the elbow. He could pop it out straight and lock it. He used that to beat Davy to death, then put it back on before your officer ever saw him."

Duggan nodded fast. This was a detail of

104

the sort a lawman was glad to know, for it narrowed the field of potential suspects considerably.

"As best I can figure out, Slick Davy had robbed One-arm sometime recently, and One-arm didn't like it. He came after Davy to settle the score."

"He did a good job of it."

"He was ready to kill me, though. Because I'd witnessed him beating Slick Davy to death. I suppose he figured that would be considered a murder. And I suppose it was . . . though if he hadn't come in when he did, I'd be a guest of the local undertaker by now."

"I'm told you are a writer by trade."

"I am."

"Well, Leadville seems to be giving you experience worth writing about."

"This last one I think I'd as soon forget."

"Will you be in town for a time, sir?"

"I will."

"You are a witness to two murders, after all, one of Calvert, the other of Slick Davy."

I nodded. It sounded hard to believe when he said it straight out like that, but it was true. I'd been doing nothing more than walking a town, looking for Josephus Mc-Cade, only to find myself tied to a post and watching two men die. Hard to fathom. It didn't seem real.

"You've held yourself together quite well, talking these things over," Duggan told me, rising. "You have some nerve about you. Have you considered law enforcement?"

"I actually have some experience at it. I helped out a town marshal over in Kansas a couple of years ago. He was a friend of mine."

"If you ever decide to leave the writing trade behind and want to work as a policeman, come talk to me. I have a feeling you could handle the work."

"I'm honored, Marshal."

"Stay in town for a time. There may be more questions. And watch out for the footpads. Slick Davy was an admired figure to some of them. To men like that, worst of the worst is best of the worst, if you know what I mean."

"I think I do."

"Good day."

A thought rose. "Marshal, one moment . . . there's a man I believe to be in town, name of Joe McCade, or Josephus McCade. He and I knew each other years ago. Have you by chance run across him? He's prone to take a drink every now and then."

"I don't believe so, sir. But if I do, I'll be

glad to inform you."

"I'm at the Swayze. One more question . . . unrelated to that one: the traveling actors who were arrested . . . are they still in custody?"

"Let 'em go two or three hours ago with the understanding they get out of town right away. Last I heard they were rolling up the road toward Gambletown. And I'm glad to see them go. We've got trouble enough in Leadville without a bunch of whores pretending to be performers."

"Whores . . . is that what they are?"

"Oh, yes. They put on an indecent show, then the real work begins."

I had nothing to say. The thought of Kathleen's younger sister being involved in prostitution unsettled me. I couldn't make myself believe it.

"Why'd you ask about that bunch of rabble?"

"I met one of the actresses. Not in any immoral or illegal way, just a chance meeting. I had an impression of her that makes it hard to think of her as what you say she is." That was all I said to him. I saw no reason to mention Katrina Ashe to him. It really wasn't his affair.

"Well, folks can fool you sometimes. Any other questions for me?"

"No."

"We'll have a few more for you later on, I'm sure. And I've got a warning for you. This one-armed fellow is still out there, and even though we're wise to him now, he may yet want to get rid of you. You be careful of him."

"I've already thought about that, Marshal."

"I doubt you'll see him, though. He won't linger about town now. Too easy to identify a man with a wooden arm. But caution is always advisable. For now, Mr. Wells, good day, and I hope those bruises heal fast."

In the shape I was in, there was no option for me but the hotel and bed. It took me half an hour just to work my way across town, every muscle sore, my joints wrenched and aching, my head pounding. I drew a lot of stares and a few people avoided me on the boardwalks. When I reached my room at last and looked into the mirror, I understood why. My ordeal with Slick Davy had left some deep tracks behind.

I fell into the bed and lay there, hurting and dejected, but glad at a deeper level to be alive. The horror I had witnessed in that cellar, the pure human brutality, first of Slick Davy and then of the one-armed man who'd beaten him to death, made me cognizant in a new way of life and its value.

It also sickened me. As I drifted away into sleep, dreams came, memories really . . . I was hanging from that spike again, awaiting death at the hands of Slick Davy. I was watching Calvert dying on the floor, then Davy himself, suffering and dying . . . his killer coming toward me . . .

I sat up with a muffled yell. Darkness. I'd slept on past the sunset, into the night.

Sitting up, I fired up a lamp and stared into the flame. What a day this had been! I couldn't recall a worse one since Andersonville.

I stared at the lamp for nearly an hour, letting my thoughts flow where they would, feeling my heart beat and my lungs fill and empty, reminding me each time that I was alive. Life was hard, life sometimes handed up horrible things. It had taken my fiancée, given me misery during wartime, the agony of Andersonville during captivity. It had left me alone and often lonely in the life I lived today. Yet it was good. To almost lose life made a man aware of how sweet and good it really was.

At length the oil began to run low, the flame to flicker. I blew it out and slept. There were no more dreams.

■ ■ ■ ■

Perhaps it was a result of my head being pounded so roughly more than once. Perhaps it was the sheer sense of draining exhaustion that comes from looking over the edge of death's brink. Perhaps it was something in the air. Whatever the cause, I slept the night through and well into the morning, utterly unaware of the sun beating against the outside of my room's closed curtains.

A thumping on the door finally broke through the murk of sleep. I opened my eyes and stared blankly across the room. The thumping came again. I rose and staggered to the door, only then realizing that I'd never undressed. I was still clad in the same clothing I'd worn as I stumbled across town the day before, head throbbing and spinning.

Baudy Wash, the cemetery tender, was at the door. "Hello, Mr. Wells, sir. I been sent to give you this."

He handed me a telegram.

"It come for you yesterday evening."

"I thought you made your living tending the graveyard, Baudy."

"Can't make much of a living with that

110

alone. I do all I can, sir, including running telegrams."

I reached into my pocket and found some change, which I turned over to Baudy. "Thank you, sir." He paused. "I must say, sir, that you're looking sickly. Are you well?"

"I almost got killed yesterday."

"No! I'm mighty sorry. I'm glad you didn't get killed."

"Me too. I hope it's a long time before you have to dig my grave, Baudy."

"Me too, sir. I'm getting mighty afraid of graves." Baudy cleared his throat and looked down the hall. "It happened again, sir."

"What?"

"The grave got dug again. This time all the way down to the box . . . and the box was busted open."

"What? Are you telling me the truth?"

"I wish I wasn't, sir. For it was the most awful-looking, awful-smelling thing you could ever see."

"Did you tell Marshal Duggan?"

"I told a policeman. He and two others come out and wrote down a bunch of notes and studied footprints and such, then covered it all back over again."

"You figure your 'ghost' came back and dug in its own grave, like before?"

"I don't know, sir. I didn't see it this time,

so I don't know."

"Baudy, why would anyone be so determined to dig up a grave? Only two reasons I can think of. Either they want to know for sure that the person in the grave is who the marker says they are, or they're looking for something that might be on or with the body."

"I wouldn't know, sir. All I know is what I've told you."

"Thanks for the information, and the telegram."

"I hope you get to doing better, sir. You don't look much better than what the man in the grave did right at the moment."

"I'm fortunate that I'm not in a grave. Somebody tried hard to put me in one."

Baudy had had enough of all this. He tipped his slouch hat, pocketed his money, and headed down the hall.

I closed the door and read Monty's telegram.

9

When I'd been with him last, Monty had complimented my writing skill. If he'd been present while I read that telegram, I'd have complimented him in turn. He'd worked on this one a while, choosing his words for brevity. Even so, this telegram must have been a chore for the key operator. It ran to four pages.

The telegram confirmed what I'd already come to suspect, and gave me further facts besides. Indeed Monty's inspection of the artwork we'd retrieved from McCade's Island turned up the rest of the letter of which I had one page, and others, too. Letters from Spencer McCade, urging his brother, Josephus, to come to him in Lake County, Colorado, so that together they could forget old differences and become mining partners. They would forget the treasure forever, just let it go. There was no hope of finding it without both his key and

Josephus's, and the latter was forever lost.

I paused after I read that. There were two keys, not just the one Josephus had lost. Two keys — whatever that meant — that were both required if the treasure — whatever that was — was to be found.

The telegram went on to say that Monty had done some legwork after receiving my wire. He'd talked to denizens of the river who had known Josephus well and conversed with him frequently. Josephus had mentioned to two or three of them that he had a brother — a twin, in fact — with whom he had experienced a major falling out just before the war. But someday, after he found his lost key, he and his brother would get together again, he'd told his fellow river rats. They'd have to, if they wanted to have the treasure.

Monty threw in one further note: one of the letters had made mention of gold.

I thought it all over.

Twin brothers, probably looking much alike. Enough alike that when Josephus had dug into the grave of his brother, a superstitious graveyard worker named Baudy had perceived him as the dead man himself, come back to life to dig in his own burial place.

But why would Josephus dig up his own

114

brother's corpse?

Simple. He was looking for his brother's key.

But what good would it do him? The two "keys," which I still assumed were keys in the metaphorical rather than literal sense, apparently were only good when used together. And Josephus's key was lost.

Or maybe not. Maybe, by some miracle, he'd actually found it after more than a decade of searching. Found his missing key and headed at once for Colorado to reconcile with his brother so that together they could claim their treasure.

But he'd come too late. Spencer McCade was dead and buried before Josephus ever arrived. And Spencer's key . . . who knew where it might be? Maybe buried with him. And so Josephus had done the unthinkable. He'd dug up his own twin brother's grave, looking for that missing key.

I wondered if he'd found it.

There was a lot of speculation in this, but I was convinced I was right. The pieces fit; they made sense.

The telegram did a lot for me, distracting me from my aches and pains and filling me with a renewed purpose. Though the most sensible place for me was bed, resting and healing, I was too intrigued by this new information to simply lie around.

I cleaned up a bit, dressed in fresh clothing, and left the hotel. I bought a big breakfast in the nearest café, then headed for a bathhouse, where I let warm water soothe my battered frame and ease the aches. Then I dressed and headed out to further pursue the mystery of Josephus McCade and his treasure.

I had a strong feeling I was going to have to completely rewrite my novel.

The undertaker was a small fellow named Harvey Soams. He was twitchy and nervous, eyes somewhat bugged and in constant motion, the beginnings of a goiter showing on his neck. He preferred to present himself primarily as a furniture maker and only secondarily as an undertaker, but I suspected the larger part of his income came from his work with the dead . . . and from selling coffins and wooden grave crosses to their families.

I could tell right off that he wasn't one to quickly give his trust. I'd come to him on the pretext of looking for a table, introduced myself, then worked the conversation away from tables and around to the subject I was really interested in. At first he was evasive, then as he warmed to me a little, began to open up.

"I deal with quite a few, you know," he said. "Folks die here all the time, same as anywhere else. I can't always remember specific ones."

"This one was fairly recent, though. Spencer McCade. You're bound to have been the one who made his grave cross, and probably his coffin."

"Just a pine box in his case. No money on him, no kin."

"So you do remember."

"Yeah, I think I do. What of him? Just another old gin fiend who got himself killed."

"Killed? It wasn't a natural death?"

He cleared his bulging throat and flickered those bug eyes from side to side, very fast. "Well, depends on who you ask. You ask the marshal, he'd say it was natural. You ask me, and I'd say that little pinhole stab wound just below his left breast had something to do with it."

"He was stabbed?"

"He was. Something small, long, and sharp. No bigger than a knitting needle and probably smaller than that. The kind of thing that leaves a tiny wound and almost no blood. He'd been stabbed beneath the breast and what little blood there was had been wiped off him. He had a hairy chest and you could hardly see the wound at all. I didn't see it until I began to wash him up some. Hell, I don't even know why I bother to do that with these pauper deaths. Ain't nobody around to care if they're clean or not."

"Darn shame for a man to die with no money. The man who makes his coffin takes a beating, eh?"

"The city pays me a pittance, just enough to cover the cost of a little bit of cheap lumber for the box. Half the time it doesn't even cover that. And I throw in the marker for free. I'm trying to get the city to pay me for those, too, where your paupers are concerned, but they're balking so far."

"You're clearly a conscientious man," I said, because I could sense he was the sort to enjoy flattery. Bug-eyed little goiter men who handled the dead all the time probably didn't get a lot of praise and compliments. "I salute you for it. You take the trouble to clean up the dead, even the paupers, and give them a decent burial and a grave marker, even though you make nothing from it."

"I try to do the decent thing." Eyes right, left, right, left . . .

"What do you care about this old dead

pauper?" he asked. His bulging eyes brightened all at once. "You kin of his?"

He was sniffing around for some proper payment, I figured. "No. But I think there might be a relative in town now."

"If you find him, you send him my way. I could stand a bit more remuneration. But if you ain't kin, why are you asking about him?" His eyes narrowed, as much as they could. "You don't know nothing about how he came to have that wound, do you?"

"I've got a theory," I said. "But if you mean, did I have anything to do with it, no, I didn't. Have you told the marshal about that wound you found on the body?"

"Nah. What's the point? Your lower breed of folks kill each other right and left around here. The fellow probably had it coming."

"Tell me this, then: was there anything unusual in the possession of the dead man?"

He looked wary all at once. "What do you mean?"

"I'm guessing it might have been a small piece of pipe, closed at both ends. Maybe tied on a string around his neck or in a pocket." This was very speculative on my part. Even though I now knew that both Josephus and his brother had "keys" to that treasure, I didn't know if Spencer's was kept in the same fashion as Josephus's.

"I don't know nothing about anything like that. I pass on everything I find on them to the marshal for whatever disposition they give to such rubbish. Generally they keep it a couple of months, then throw it out, or auction it if it's worth it."

Sometimes you can just tell when a man is lying. This fellow probably supplemented his income by pilfering the pocket change and small possessions of Leadville's dead. And it seemed to me that a look of recognition had fired up in those shifty eyes of his when I described what I was looking for.

"Anything else I can do for you, sir?" he asked.

"No. Thank you for your time." I shook the hand of this handler of corpses and wondered how often he washed it.

Outside, I paused near the window. The shutter was partly ajar. I peeked in and watched undertaker Harvey Soams unlocking and opening a cabinet on the wall. He produced a wooden box, set it on the table, and began pulling from it assorted change purses, pocket knives, jewelry, and the like. He then lifted out a small piece of metal pipe, tied on a string and enclosed at both ends. He held it up and stared at it, put it to his ear and shook it.

There it was: Spencer McCade's "key,"

the counterpart of the one Josephus Mc-Cade had lost in '65.

I held my breath as I watched Soams examining the item. *Don't pocket it,* I mentally urged him. *Put it back in the box.*

He did. And the box went back into the cabinet, which he closed and locked.

Soams came toward the window. I ducked away and around the corner, into an alley. I heard him close the shutter, then a moment later heard the door close. He walked by, never noticing me back in the shadows.

When he was gone I went to the door and found it unlocked. People probably weren't prone to enter this place, not while they were alive, anyway. Entering the room, I quickly popped the small lock on the cabinet, took out the box, and from it removed the piece of enclosed pipe.

If this was theft, it wasn't one that plagued my conscience. Soams had no more right to own this item than I did. And I actually had a chance to do something good with it, assuming there really might be something to this treasure business. If I could find Josephus McCade, I could give it to him. And if he'd actually found his own lost "key," he might be able to claim his treasure at last.

I put everything back in place, leaving it as it had been, except of course for the cabinet having been sprung. Soams would be livid when he discovered that someone had been into his private little place, but what could he say? This cabinet contained items he'd stolen, things that properly should belong either to the families of various deceased people or to the city of Leadville. Given the line of my questions to him, he'd certainly suspect me of being the culprit. Let him suspect. There was nothing he could say or do.

I shook the little piece of pipe near my ear. Sure enough, there was something inside, not heavy. It made a sliding, shifting sound. A piece of tightly rolled paper, I suspected. I wondered what it said, and why Spencer McCade had never sawed open this pipe to find out for himself.

It was tempting to do so myself, but I resisted. This was not my possession, just something I was safekeeping until I could find Josephus McCade.

I slipped the string around my neck and tucked the piece of pipe away under my shirt. It lay cool and heavy against my chest.

Wouldn't it be intriguing to know what was inside it? It was going to be hard to resist the temptation to find out. Resist the devil, and he'll flee from you, the Bible says.

But it's hard when the devil is tied on a string and hanging around your neck.

10

Nightfall. The busy world of Leadville mining gave way to the equally busy world of Leadville entertainment. I sat near the door of a combination saloon and dance hall, sipping a beer and studying the item I'd taken from the undertaker's cabinet.

A dozen questions scrambled around my head, each touching off theories and imaginations, each planting the seeds of possible stories I might write. I now felt I had to locate Josephus McCade, if only to find out the truth about him and his treasure, and to learn what were these "keys" that he and his estranged brother had possessed.

Who had created these "keys"? Were they maps, portions of maps, written narrative that told the way to treasure? Why was it necessary to have both of them together to use them? Why had they been given to the McCade brothers, and by whom?

I had to know.

But there was now much more to this than personal curiosity. If the undertaker was right, Josephus's brother had been murdered. Josephus had a right to know that.

Who had killed him? In a town like this, full of footpads and people on the run from the law back East, it could have been anyone. If Spencer had been prone to drink, like his brother, he'd probably moved in rough and rowdy circles.

The motive could have been anything. But probably not theft, otherwise the "key" would have been taken. But no, not necessarily. Why would any sensible thief take a piece of pipe on a string? No obvious inherent value there.

Dropping the bit of pipe back under my shirt, I looked up just in time to see a familiar figure walk past the open door of the dance hall. Margaret Rains, the actress I'd met when I trounced Slick Davy in the alley, and who had sent me that letter about Katrina Ashe.

What was she doing in Leadville? Marshal Duggan had told me the actors had been run out of town.

If she was still here, maybe Katrina Ashe was as well. I rose, taking my hat from the table, leaving money in its place. I headed out the door and turned right.

She was already out of sight, lost in the evening foot traffic of Leadville. I walked through this town of scent and color and motion, looking for her. There she was, turning a corner. I hurried my pace to close the gap.

"Card game, mister? You look lucky tonight." Just a boy, not old enough to shave, flashing a deck at me, grinning. The odds of me winning whatever game he offered were about equal to the chance the moon would fall into the Rocky Mountains and bounce over to California. I pushed on past.

Around the corner, I'd lost her again. A wagon rolled by, and beyond it I saw her, just reaching the other side of the street. I trotted onto the street after her, dodging a sizable memento left by a passing horse, then opened my mouth to call out her name.

I didn't do so, however, because a man appeared. He was on a porch, back against a storefront and initially out of sight. He stepped forward to meet her. She stopped, spoke to him a few moments. He lost his grin, shook his head. She talked some more, just a little louder. There was a mention of money. He frowned at her, said something I could not make out but which sounded harsh. She replied, softer this time, and he softened as well. His grin came back; he nodded. She slipped her arm into his and they walked down the street together, then entered a very cheap-looking, run-down hotel.

I didn't know this woman, not really, and already had been under no illusions about her character. She was a player in a deliberately indecent stage performance, after all. But it made me feel a bit sick to see her actually negotiating for an act of prostitution. The letter she'd sent me had revealed a certain style and class, almost an elegance. The concern it had revealed for Katrina had been touching. Her manner in our one face-to-face meeting had impressed me. She was better than what she was doing right now.

And if she was doing this, was it not likely Katrina was doing the same?

Kathleen was gone forever; I could not have her back. But some of her soul lived on in her sister, surely. If she was involved in the same kind of life as Margaret Rains . . .

Margaret Rains had written that Katrina was in a "troubling" situation and in need of help. I vowed that I would find her, whether she was still in Leadville, like Margaret, or had gone on to Gambletown as the marshal had indicated.

Feeling troubled I simply walked, circling

around Leadville, worrying about Katrina and at the same time keeping my eye out for Josephus McCade.

Odd, how what had started out as a routine trip to visit the family of an Andersonville survivor had turned into something much more complex.

I was pondering all this when my path brought me back around to the same spot from which I'd watched Margaret Rains head into the hotel. Now from that same hotel erupted a loud, feminine scream. It jolted me out of my reverie and stopped me in my tracks.

A second scream. It sounded to me like Margaret Rains's voice.

"What was that?" asked a man nearby me.

"I don't know . . . let's go see," I said.

"Uh-uh. Not me." He turned and was gone.

Alone, I ran to the hotel and pushed through the door. There was another scream, coming from the floor above.

"Can I help you, mister?" the clerk demanded.

"It's not me who needs help, from the sound of it," I said, heading up the stairs.

"Hold on, you!" the clerk hollered.

Ignoring him, I reached the second floor. At the far end of the hall a door opened and Margaret Rains stumbled out, her right arm extended behind her. She was dressed in a petticoat, her dress crumpled in her left hand. Her hair was disheveled and there was a long, bleeding scratch down the side of her face.

I saw why her right arm was extended behind her. The same man I'd seen her negotiating with on the street had her wrist in his grasp and was trying to pull her back into the room. His face was dark as a storm cloud and he was cursing very robustly.

"You there!" I shouted at him. "Let her go!"

Neither he nor she had noticed me. He paid no heed to me now, but Margaret reacted at once. She looked at me with a face full of fear and pleading.

"He's going to kill me!" she yelled.

The man yanked her, turning her around and almost dragging her back into his room. He was clad only in long underwear. I reached them, drew back my fist, and drove it into his chin as he turned to see who was butting into his business.

He let her go at once, staggered backward, and fell straight down like a building whose foundation just crumbled.

"Are you all right?" I asked her.

"He . . . he was going to . . . he tried . . ."

129

"No need to talk about it."

"He hit me . . . I think he would have killed me!"

"Come on. Let's get you out of here before the sleeper awakens."

"Thank God you were here! How did you know?"

"You've got a good loud scream. Let's go."

The door across the hall opened; a drunken man staggered out. He stared at the unconscious man on the floor. "Hey? Is he dead?"

"Nope," I said. "Just taking a rest and thinking about his wicked ways."

"Huh!" He stumbled across the hall and over the fallen man. He found the man's pants discarded on the floor and began rifling the pockets.

Margaret paused at the end of the hall and put on her dress. She was shaking and crying.

"Miss Rains, I suggest you try hard to find a safer line of work," I said.

She suddenly became an offended and angry creature. "Don't preach to me!" she snapped. "You don't know what I've gone through in my life! You don't know what makes a person do what they do!" Then at once her face changed and she wept again. "I'm sorry," she said. "You're right . . .

you're right. I'm sorry. You've saved me, and I shouldn't be harsh with you. I should only thank you."

"I doubt I saved you. You'd have gotten away from him yourself," I said. But I didn't believe it.

"I want to go where he won't find me."

"I thought you and your troupe were in Gambletown. The marshal told me you'd gone there . . . that you'd been more or less asked to leave town."

"Why were you talking to the marshal about us?"

"It wasn't really about you. It was something else and the matter of your troupe just came up. But why aren't you in Gambletown with the others?"

We were walking through the lobby at this point. The desk clerk was giving me a hard look, but didn't say anything. When we reached the door Margaret all but ran out.

"I stayed here because of *him.*" She waved back at the hotel we'd just left.

"You'd set up an . . . arrangement with him already?"

"Yes. I wish I hadn't. I thought he was going to kill me. I've never met a man like him. He seemed to take pleasure in the idea of . . . killing me. What's wrong with people that they get so twisted sometimes?"

131

"The pure human capacity for evil, that's why. I've seen plenty of it myself, in all kinds of forms. Miss Rains, truly you've got to find a new way to make a living."

"I know. I know."

"Let's go to my hotel. I'll rent you a room there. We'll use a false name and no one will know. He'll not be able to find you if he comes looking. Do you think he will come looking?"

"I don't know. No. I don't think so. Thank God you were close by."

"Thank God you know how to raise a ruckus," I said.

There was no room available at the hotel. The looks I received from the clerk as I inquired let me know what his perception of the situation was. I didn't care. I'd been through far too much in my time to be much concerned with the perceptions of others.

"I'll go . . . I'll find a place to stay on my own," she said.

"Nonsense," I replied. "You'll stay in my room. There's a porch just outside it, with chairs. I'll take a blanket out there and sleep."

"I can't do that. I can't impose and take your bed."

"It's not my bed tonight. It's yours. I ask only one thing: tell me what kind of problem Katrina is having."

She hesitated, then nodded. "All right. I don't think she would object."

"Is she in Gambletown?"

"Yes."

"Is she doing . . . the same thing you have been doing?"

Margaret looked away. "Yes."

I nodded. "Well . . . I guess then . . ." And I found I had nothing to say.

"Are you sure you don't mind giving up your room? I mean . . . if you want to sleep on the bed . . . I'm not talking of the kind of thing you may first think . . . I mean . . ."

"I understand. Thank you, but no. I think a night out on the porch might do me some good. Fresh air and all."

"You saved my life tonight."

"That's a bit of a stretcher. I think you'd have gotten away from him. But the next one, you don't know. And there may not be anyone around to help."

"I know."

"Come on. I'll show you the room."

I sat on a hard and uncomfortable chair on the second-story hotel porch, wearing a jacket and my hat, plus a blanket thrown across me, in a vain attempt to keep warm in a night that had turned chilly. Inside my room, Margaret Rains slept, no doubt much more comfortable and warm than I was.

But discomfort wasn't on my mind. Margaret had told me of the trouble that was on the heels of the young woman who would have been my sister-in-law. And it shook me, because I wasn't quite sure how to help.

I leaned back in the chair, mulling it over, staring at the sky, and at times watching those who passed on the street below. This was not a busy part of town — my logic in choosing a hotel not very close to any saloon or dance hall was proving itself out — but that only seemed to make those who did pass all the more noticeable.

I myself was substantially invisible from the street below. The building was dark and all around it were dark, and the moon tonight was mostly hidden by clouds. I was an invisible, watching ghost in the darkness . . . a ghost who appeared unlikely to get much sleep tonight.

But I did sleep, at least sporadically, because I felt myself jerk awake as I almost slid out of the chair. Sitting up, I looked around. The town was brighter, the moon having emerged from the clouds. It had moved across the sky and was now a small point of bright light.

Standing, I stretched and paced about a little, trying to ease a cramp in my leg. As I did so I realized I had an audience. A man across the street, under a porch overhang, was looking at me. At first I assumed it was a policeman who found it curious and probably suspicious that a man would be pacing about on a hotel porch at such an hour. When I looked at him, however, he moved back farther under the porch overhang, then turned and walked at a rapid pace back up toward the busier and more rowdy part of town.

It was Josephus McCade, and he was gone as quickly as I realized it.

Doubt hit me. I could hardly be sure he was McCade. I'd not seen him since Andersonville, and besides, bright moonlight or not, this was nighttime and there hid distance between me and the man I'd seen with my sleep-clouded eyes.

None of that persuaded me. McCade had been a distinctive fellow with a distinctive gait, and I was all but certain that I'd just seen him. Moreover, I think he himself had found something familiar about me, given the way he had been studying me from that hidden spot.

I was already dressed, except for my boots, which sat beside the chair. I put them on hurriedly. My pistol . . . inside the room. No time to get it. I headed for the side of the porch, swung down over the rail, then dropped to the street below.

With any luck I'd catch up to him. My opportunity to meet Josephus McCade might be at hand.

11

Fortune was with me. I quickly spotted Josephus McCade, heading at a fast pace into one of the saloons that ran all night.

My second sighting of him confirmed that this was indeed McCade. I'd talked to him a few times at Andersonville and had seen him walking across the prison yard a thousand times. He was older now, and a little bit heavier — though not much — but he was definitely the same man.

I stepped up to the door of the saloon and looked in before entering. McCade was at the bar, ordering a drink. He fidgeted while he waited for it, drumming his fingers on the top of the bar. When then drink arrived he downed it quickly, then hammered the bottom of the glass on the bar to call the barkeep back again.

I slipped in the door and sat down at a nearby table. McCade seemed so edgy that I hesitated to approach him directly. I'd watch him a little longer first.

The barkeep seemed hesitant this time. A question about McCade's ability to pay, most likely, and I didn't blame him: McCade looked like a man who'd spent the last dozen years living on an island in the Mississippi. McCade argued with him, his words hard to make out because of other noise in the barroom, and eventually the barkeep relented and gave him a second drink.

This one McCade sipped slowly. He turned and looked around the room. I reflexively lowered my head and pretended to pick at a hangnail, letting the brim of my hat cover my face.

When I looked up again, McCade looked like he'd been struck ill. He had an expression of great fear on his face, mouth agape, eyes wide. I followed his gaze. He was looking at a man who stood at the bat-winged saloon door, looking into the room just as I had moments before. I expect my own expression changed as well. This was the one-armed man who had killed Slick Davy, and very nearly killed me.

He entered the saloon. My heart started up again. This was an entirely different fellow, just one who looked a little like the one-armed man.

I looked up at McCade and saw a look of deep relief on his face . . . and all at once I had a moment of realization, or at least very strong suspicion.

It all hinged on the assumption that McCade had mistaken this newcomer for the same one-armed man I had mistaken him for. On that premise, that look of fright on his face indicated he, like me, had some cause to be wary of the one-armed fellow. That indicated that McCade and the one-armed man had some history together. Bad history.

But it was only speculation. McCade might have mistaken the man in the saloon for someone other than the one-armed man. But there was one reason, at least, to think otherwise.

I recalled what that bartender at the Horsecollar Saloon in Gambletown had said: the man who had thrown the glass at that McCade drawing on the wall had moved in a strangely stiff way, and used only his left arm. He'd been described as burly, bearded, looking like a miner.

It was a perfect description of the one-armed man who'd killed Slick Davy.

The man who'd come into the saloon loudly greeted some friends in the back, and went to join them amid backslaps and coarse jokes. I watched them a moment, then turned.

McCade was gone. I looked around for him. How the devil had he vanished so quickly?

There he was . . . slipping toward a closed back door. The bartender was busy, pouring drinks for a couple of men who'd already had too much. McCade tried the door and apparently found it locked. He edged to a nearby window, which was open, and in an admirably deft bit of movement put a leg out, pulled the other one after it, and disappeared.

The scoundrel was leaving the saloon without paying his tab! I grudgingly had to admire his brass at doing it in so blatant a way. Oddly, I don't think anyone else in the place had noticed.

I'd not bought a thing here, so I simply rose and headed out the front door and around the building. I hadn't seen which way McCade had gone, so I hesitated at the back of the building, looking both directions. There were plenty of avenues for disappearance and no way to tell which he'd taken. I picked one at random.

Luck guided me. I saw him ahead, moving as quickly as ever. Maybe heading for another saloon to pull precisely the same trick.

I almost called to him. There was no reason to be cagey; I could think of no reason he'd wish to avoid me, and I needed to give him his late brother's "key" in any case.

But his manner was so furtive that I hesitated to make my presence known. He'd probably just flee. So I followed him, staying out of sight.

I came to a halt when he did. Still away from him and unnoticed, I watched him a moment, then muttered to myself, "I'll be!"

He was at the door of the undertaker's building, looking right and left to make sure he wasn't watched. He put his hand to the latch and found it locked. Another look right and left. He went to the window, elbowed out a pane, and reached inside to loosen the latch. He slid up the window, pulled himself up, and went inside.

I had to hand it to McCade. He was good with windows, both going out and going in.

It wasn't hard to guess what he was up to. He'd already dug up and searched his own brother's corpse. He was after the little bit of enclosed pipe that at this moment swung on a string around my neck.

He'd not find it inside. I'd already beat

him to that punch.

What to do? If he was caught having broken into this building, he could find some real trouble. But what if I startled him too badly, and he was armed? I didn't want to get myself shot.

Out of the gloom a figure emerged. Big, burly, bearded . . . oh, no.

He was headed for the undertaker's. Creeping toward it, really.

Obviously I wasn't the only one who'd noticed McCade.

The moon vanished behind a cloud and I lost sight of the man moving toward the building. I was nearly sure, though, that it was the one-armed man.

No question now, I had to warn McCade. I edged to the building and entered the window just as he had.

"McCade!" I whispered sharply. "McCade, I know you're in here . . . I'm Jed Wells. We met at Andersonville. Hide yourself! There's someone coming after you!"

A shadow moved by the window. I ducked. The figure paused there, looking in . . .

I'd been wrong. This wasn't the one-armed man. He wasn't even bearded . . . it had been a trick of the light.

This was one of Leadville's uniformed policemen, making rounds.

An open window with one pane broken wasn't something he'd pass up. He'd come inside, without a doubt.

Doing my best to be silent, I sneaked toward a nearby wardrobe. Maybe I could hide inside . . . but did I really want that? It would only make me look all the more guilty to be found not only inside, but hiding from the law.

Where was McCade? Had he gone out a back way, or was he in here somewhere?

Nothing to do but open up the door and let the policeman in. Just tell him the facts, or part of them: I'd seen someone enter and had come in to investigate.

It sounded unconvincing even to me, and I knew it was the truth.

The policeman reached the door. I headed toward it to let him in . . . and just then a pine coffin near the far wall moved; the lid burst up and a figure sat up.

"Who the devil!" the figure exclaimed. A match flared and revealed the face, shifting eyes, and growing goiter of Harvey Soams, undertaker and coffin builder.

The policeman hammered on the door. "Open up!" he hollered. "Open up in the name of the Leadville police!"

"You stay right there!" Soams said, lifting a pistol. The man was in a nightshirt and

143

stocking cap, a blanket draped across him.

Good Lord . . . the man slept in the coffins he made. And kept a pistol in there with him. Stranger and stranger.

"Don't shoot!" I said, spreading my hands. "I'm unarmed."

"Open up!" the policeman called from outside, hammering the door again.

"Want me to let him in?" I asked Soams.

"You!" he declared. "You're the one who was in here, asking about that Spencer McCade!"

I noticed something of significance just then. The lid of another of the coffins moved, just a little, as soon as Soams said the name of Spencer McCade. So now I knew where Josephus was hiding.

The policeman, tired of waiting, rammed the door with his shoulder, once, twice, and then a third time. The latch shattered and the policeman burst in, pistol raised.

Soams let out a yelp and dropped his match, which went out.

"Freeze still as ice!" the policeman ordered. "You there, in the box . . . strike another match!"

Soams did, though it took him a minute to succeed. When he finally had a match going, he trembled so badly he almost shook out the flame.

"Out of that coffin!" the policeman ordered.

Soams obeyed, but clumsily, dumping the coffin over in the process. He almost fell down, stumbling and bumping into me. He dropped his matches, found them, and finally got a lamp burning.

I eyed the coffin that I knew hid McCade, and wondered if he'd manage to keep quiet with all the activity in the room.

"Soams? Is that you?" the policeman asked.

"Yes . . . this one here, he broke in!" Soams said, pointing at me.

The policeman frowned. "Since when have you started sleeping in your own coffins, Soams?"

"I have a bad back," he said. "The hard coffin makes it feel better."

The policeman turned to me. "Who are you?"

"I'm Jed Wells."

"Why are you in here?"

I faced a predicament. Did I reveal McCade's presence? I didn't want to. If I didn't, though, I would be perceived as no more than a break-and-enter thief who had come in here for no good reason.

Again, maybe selective parts of the truth were what would work best.

"I came in because I saw somebody break in . . . or thought I did. I'd been in here earlier today, and met Mr. Soams. I didn't want anyone stealing from him."

"Uh-huh. Just a citizen doing his righteous duty, then," the policeman said.

"A citizen trying to do so, sir."

"I didn't hear anyone in here before I sat up and saw Wells here," Soams said.

Sound sleeper, apparently. Or maybe Mc-Cade was just exceptionally good at sneaking around in silence.

"Look around, Soams. See if anything has been stolen," the policeman said.

"All right."

Soams began looking around, opening desk drawers, looking in cabinets. Eventually he'd get around to that cabinet that I'd broken open earlier. I wondered if he'd notice the missing pipe on a string. Of course he would . . . I'd asked about that very item when I was in here before.

"Jed Wells," the policeman said. "Jed Wells . . . where have I heard that name before?"

I shrugged.

"Wait a minute . . . *The Dark Stockade.* That book about Andersonville. I read part of it. The man who wrote it was named Jed Wells."

"Is that right?"

"It isn't you, is it?"

"Do I look like a writer to you?"

He laughed.

Soams headed for the cabinet where he kept the items he took from the dead. Maybe he wouldn't want the policeman to see his cache and wouldn't bring it out.

"That wasn't much of a book, anyway," the policeman said. "Bunch of Yankee rubbish."

Soams said, "The latch on this cabinet is broken."

The policeman went over and looked at it. "It wasn't this way already?"

"No."

"What's in here?"

Soams swallowed; the goiter did a little dance. "Unclaimed personal effects from paupers and unidentified dead. Just a few things I haven't turned over to the marshal yet."

I was in trouble now. I should have realized Soams had a perfect excuse for keeping those items. If he was ever questioned about them, all he had to do was say he simply hadn't gotten around to turning them over yet. If he was never questioned about them, they were his.

Soams dragged out his box and began going through it. "There's something gone," he said.

"What's that?"

"Well, it's just a piece of pipe, closed on the ends, with a string tied around it. He was asking about it when he was in here during the day."

"Talk to me, friend," the policeman said to me.

"Why would I want a piece of pipe on a string?" I asked.

The policeman drew closer to me, squinting. "What's this?" he asked, reaching for the string around my neck.

"Just a saint's medal I wear."

"Pull it out from under your clothes. Let's see it."

I shook my head and sighed, then pulled out the piece of pipe.

"That's it!" Soams said. "He's taken it!"

The policeman looked at me with disgust. "Let's pay a visit to my office. I'd like to show you around the place. Let you stay awhile, perhaps."

"I had a tour earlier."

"How'd you get so bruised up? You been fighting?"

"Ask Marshal Duggan. I've already told him all about it. I almost got murdered by two different people, one of them a footpad

148

who didn't like the fact I'd whipped his hide, the other a one-armed man who didn't like the fact I'd witnessed him committing a murder."

"Want me to come, too?" Soams asked.

"If you can, sir. It would be helpful to have you write and sign a complaint and description of what was taken." The policeman looked at the piece of pipe. "What is this, anyway?"

"A key," I said.

"Looks like a pipe to me."

"It does at that." I spoke just a little louder. "But there's someone around Leadville just now who knows it's a key."

"Who's that?"

"He knows who he is."

"I think you are loco, sir. I question whether you are of sound mind."

"I ask the same question of myself sometimes."

"Let's go. You have some explaining you'll need to do."

"I'm not sure I can explain it, sir. And if I do, I'd like it to be to Marshal Duggan."

"Then you're prepared to spend the night in the jail, I take it. Marshal Duggan won't be back in until morning."

"Please, officer. Let me go free. I'm staying at the Swayze House. I give you my solemn word I'll come in first thing tomorrow and talk to Marshal Duggan, if you'll let me go back tonight."

"Sorry. Can't do it."

Of course he couldn't. I thought of Margaret Rains back in my hotel room. What would she think when she found me gone?

And what about Katrina Ashe? I needed to leave here, get to Gambletown, and find her, without delay.

It looked like there would be delay, like it or not. Just how long, I couldn't guess.

"Why do you want this 'key,' as you call it?" the policeman asked.

"I was planning to give it to its rightful owner," I said, hoping the rightful owner, hiding in a coffin nearby, heard me clearly.

We left the undertaker's parlor, the three of us. I figure it took Josephus McCade no more than ten seconds to vacate the place after we were gone.

The policeman did not restrain me. The thought of running came as a pleasant fantasy, but realism prevailed. I'd be shot at worst or buy myself some much deeper trouble at best.

But I did fall back a little, and speak in a whisper to Soams.

"Keep something in mind," I said. "The police might be interested in hearing about

150

an undertaker who detects that a dead man has been murdered, and says nothing of it."

His eyes bugged a little more.

"Just think about that when you make your official statement," I said.

"Get up here close to me, Wells," the policeman said. "You don't need to be talking to him."

"Sorry, officer."

I trotted up ahead and left Soams to think about what I'd said.

12

Marshal Duggan held the short piece of pipe in his hand, turning it. He shook it and held it to his ear.

"Something inside."

"Yes, sir," I said.

"It's property of the city, properly speaking."

"No, sir, not with a next of kin living."

"And who is that?"

"His name is Josephus McCade. He's spent the last decade, more than that, really, living on an island in the Mississippi River, near Memphis. At one time he had a piece of pipe similar to that one, with something inside. He managed to keep it all the way through the Andersonville prison camp — we were prisoners there together — then lost it when the *Sultana* exploded. He was on it. But the key, as he calls it, was taken before that ever happened. A man onboard, I don't know his name, took it from him.

The same man got his arm blown off in the explosion. Lost the 'key' as well. Josephus McCade spent the next dozen years searching the riverbank for it."

"Sounds crazy. The odds of finding such a thing . . ."

"He is crazy. He was already crazy at Andersonville. But even crazier than he is, is that I think he really did find the thing. I don't know how, but I think he did."

"Why?"

"Because he left his island all at once, without a word even to the people who had taken care of him for so many years. And he came here, to Leadville, to find a brother he'd been estranged from for years. Spencer McCade."

"The one buried in the cemetery."

"That's right. And if you'll talk to Baudy Wash, who digs the graves and tends the graveyard —"

"I know Baudy."

"— Baudy will tell you all about seeing a dead man digging in his own grave. Trying to dig himself up. He ran off when Baudy showed up. But he came back another time and did it again. This time he got the grave all the way open, and opened the box, too."

"Wait a minute . . . there's a report filed in this office about something like that."

"Baudy called in some policeman when he found the grave open."

"The right thing to do. What was that about a man digging in his own grave?"

"What Baudy saw was Josephus McCade digging in the grave of his twin brother. You can imagine how confusing and frightening that would be, if you tended a lonely old cemetery, surrounded by the dead all the time. You look out one night, and there's a man who is the spitting image of a man you saw buried, and he's digging in the grave of that man."

"A dead man digging in his own grave."

"That's how it would appear."

"Looking for what?"

"For what you have in your hand. Josephus didn't know it had been taken off the body, I suppose. I guess he might have thought paupers were just dumped into a box, clothes and personal effects and all, and simply buried. Of course, he didn't find that little piece of pipe on his brother's corpse. He didn't realize that the undertaker had already removed it."

"So why didn't he go to the undertaker to ask for it?"

He had, in his own way, this very night. But McCade apparently wasn't so much the asking kind as the break-and-enter kind.

"He might do that yet," I said. "He'll probably figure out soon enough that the undertaker might have his brother's little toy."

"So this thing here, put together with the one that the living brother has, or maybe has . . ."

"Apparently is the key to finding something of value. Maybe some gold. I don't know much about that part."

"Maybe you want this gold for yourself, Mr. Wells. Maybe that's why you broke into the coroner's office to find this thing."

"I did enter, but I didn't break in. That had already been done by somebody else."

"Uh-huh. So where was this 'somebody else' when my officer went in after you?"

"I figure he'd gone out another door, or a window. Maybe he was hiding inside somewhere."

"Or maybe there never was such a person. After all, it was your neck that this string was tied around."

"I've got a confession to make, Marshal. I did take this, but not tonight. Earlier."

"Is that right? Explain."

I told him of watching Soams look in the cabinet and remove the very item he'd denied was in there. I admitted that I'd walked back in the place after Soams walked out, broke the cabinet open, and took the piece of pipe.

"I did it because it isn't rightfully Soams's property, or even the city's. It belongs to Josephus McCade. I had it in mind to give it to him when I finally find him."

"Or maybe you have it in mind to take the counterpart that he has, and go after that treasure for yourself."

"I can see how you'd think that. But money isn't much important to me, Marshal. I've made some good money already, through the writing trade. I've got another book in the works that will make me even more. In fact, one of the central characters in that new book is based on one Josephus McCade. And that's the main reason I want to find him. I want to know him better, because if I do, I'll write a better book for it."

"And you're just going to hand him this piece of pipe."

"That was my plan."

"Tell me this: why did you take such a personal interest when you saw this stranger breaking into the undertaker's parlor tonight? Most people would have just told a policeman."

"You know, the reason I did what I did was that the person looked like it might be

Josephus McCade. Now that I think about it, though, I don't think it was."

"You don't think so, eh?"

"No, sir."

Duggan stood and paced back and forth, unspeaking for about half a minute. "Let me tell you what I think, sir. I think that you're a man who is prone to find trouble, or maybe it's trouble that finds you. All I know about you is that you say you're Jed Wells, and that you write books. All I know about you is that we found you strung up to a post in a room with two dead footpads, telling tales about a man who beat one of the two to death with his own wooden arm. Your story, wild as it sounds, is believable because of the situation we found you in, and your injuries. But now, here we find you in an undertaker's parlor in the middle of the night, telling stories about following thieves in through broken windows, all because you want to be a good citizen."

"No. I did it because I thought I saw Josephus McCade go in through the window. I've been wanting to find that man, and I didn't want to see him get in trouble breaking into a place looking for something I already had."

"I don't know what to make of you, sir. I don't know whether to tell you to stay around town so I can keep an eye on you, or just run you out of town so I don't have to find you in the middle of some new piece of trouble tomorrow night or the next." All of a sudden he stopped, thinking hard. "Wait a minute . . . you said the man who beat Slick Davy to death had one arm. And you said the man who took this Joe Mc-Cade's piece of pipe on the boat lost an arm in the process."

"I think the two may be one and the same. I don't know it, but I suspect it. You see, Josephus McCade is an artist, a good one. He paid for some drinks he had in a saloon up in Gambletown by drawing a picture of the *Sultana* on the wall. The owner liked it so much that he covered it over with glass to protect it. Then in comes a big man with a beard and a right arm that hangs unmoving at his side — like a wooden arm — and he looks over that piece of art and smashes the glass that covers it. Sounds to me like somebody with a bad attitude about Josephus McCade and the *Sultana*."

"You think he's looking for McCade?"

There was more I could have told him. I could have told him that I had a sneaking suspicion that the one-armed man might have already found one McCade . . . Spencer McCade. And when he found him, he probably thought that Spencer was actually Josephus. The two looked alike, after all.

But I didn't share this theory with Duggan. For one thing, I couldn't prove it. For another, I wanted to hold as an ace up my sleeve the fact that Soams had detected that a dead pauper had been murdered rather than dying a natural death, and failed to report this to the authorities as required by law. For yet another, I didn't have a lot of confidence in my theory, just an instinctive sense it might be correct. But there were gaps in it that I couldn't fit together right away. If One-arm had killed Spencer McCade because he thought he was killing Josephus McCade, he surely would have done so only because he wanted to get the key again. So why had the key still been on Spencer's body when it was turned over to Soams?

I really had no proof at all that the one-armed man had killed Spencer. But it was an intriguing possibility, especially given the similarity of appearance between the McCade brothers.

The policeman who had arrested me knocked on the door and was admitted. He called Duggan aside and spoke to him in a low tone.

Duggan returned looking bemused. "Well,

it appears that Mr. Soams and his goiter have been having a talk with each other, and have decided they don't want to make an issue of this. He says he's willing to let the whole thing go, if you'll replace the broken window, repair the broken cabinet, and fix the door."

"The door was the work of your own policeman, not me."

"Still . . ."

"It's not a problem. I'll leave the money with you."

"Fair enough. Consider yourself a lucky man, Mr. Wells. And keep in mind that I could make trouble for you over this even if Soams doesn't want to."

"Is that your plan?"

"Nope. But I do plan to keep an eye on you."

"I might need to leave town, make a trip to Gambletown."

"Let that trip wait awhile, Mr. Wells. I want to have you ready at hand should we make any arrests of one-armed men or sketch-drawing lunatics."

I nodded, but I knew I couldn't accommodate that command. I had to get to Gambletown and Katrina Ashe, no matter what Marshal Duggan thought of it.

"What about the piece of pipe there?" I asked.

Duggan picked it up. "It's property of the city pending being claimed by the rightful owner. I'll keep it here. If you run across this McCade, tell him where he can find it."

"I'll do that."

"I might like the chance to talk to him a bit, myself. It's not legal to dig up graves and search corpses, you know."

Outside, I saw Soams standing and smoking a hand-rolled cigarette. I approached him.

"Thanks for deciding not to make an issue of things."

"What can a man do when he's threatened like you threatened me?"

"I didn't say anything about Spencer McCade's stab wound. And I don't intend to. Except to his brother, who has a right to know it."

"If that man goes to the law and tells about it, I'll deny I ever noticed the wound."

"I doubt it will come to that. The two brothers have been estranged. His interest in finding him had more to do with mercenary spirit than brotherly love, I suspect."

"Mr. Wells, I'd appreciate it if you'd stay clear of me from now on."

"You can count on it, sir. Have a good

day. And get yourself a real bed. It's down-right . . . strange, sleeping in a casket."

"We'll all sleep in one someday."

"No point in rushing it."

13

I'm not sure why it did not surprise me to find Margaret Rains gone. I think I would have been more surprised to find her still there. Little opportunity had come for me to get to know her well, but my impression was of a woman at the mercy of changing circumstances and changing moods. For all I knew, she was out right now engaging again in prostitution. Or maybe she was on her way to Gambletown, assuming I'd abandoned her.

She'd not taken anything from my room, anyway. Whatever else she was, she wasn't a thief.

It angered me that she'd left. What if she encountered that same man I'd left unconscious on his hotel room floor?

Good Lord . . . what if he'd come to the hotel and taken her away?

I shut off that thought. I had enough to think about with Katrina alone.

I readied myself for a short journey and headed out to the livery.

I was saddling my horse when I became conscious of someone behind me. Silently watching. I turned.

For a few moments Josephus McCade and I simply looked at one another.

"Hello, McCade," I said. "Good to see you again."

"I know you," he said. "I remember you from . . . the place I wish I'd never been."

"Yeah. Me too." I advanced to him and put out my hand. He reached over and shook it. "Glad to see you got out of that burying box all right."

"You knew I was there?"

"I saw the lid move. Nobody else did. Maybe you could tell that some of the things I said, I said for your sake."

"I thought so." He stared at me. "You look younger than you did at Andersonville."

"Everybody who was at Andersonville looks younger now than they did then. Those lucky enough to survive."

"In the undertaker's, you talked about my brother. You talked about the pipe on the string. You talked about a one-armed man."

"I did. I wanted you to hear it all. I've followed your trail for a long way. All the way from your island near Memphis."

"You following me?"

"It wasn't on purpose. I came for another purpose, which ended up coming to nothing. Then I learned you had a brother here, and when I saw the art you did on the wall in that saloon in Gambletown, I knew you were here."

"How'd you know?"

"I'm familiar with your art, Mr. McCade. I remember it from Andersonville, and I saw plenty of it on your island. Montford Wilks has most of it now. He took it to protect it."

"He's a good man. He's been kind to me for years. When I'm rich I'm going to share it with him."

"I doubt he'd take it. He's got plenty of money already."

"Why were you on my island?"

"I'm a writer, Josephus. Can I call you Josephus?"

"Call me Joe. It's shorter."

"All right, Joe. I was on your island because I was visiting Monty Wilks. I've written a book, and there's a man in it who is something like you. Not you, but inspired by you. Monty told me about your island and that you'd gone missing. We went to take a look for ourselves. They all thought you were dead, Joe, the way you'd disappeared so fast."

"I ain't dead. I was just in a hurry to go, that's all."

"There were some letters there. You'd used the backs for drawing paper. That's how we figured out you had a brother in Leadville."

"Had. Ain't got one no more. He's dead. But you know that."

"I do. Joe, he was murdered. Did you know that?"

"Murdered?"

"Stuck in the heart with some sort of sharp pick."

"God."

"Sorry to have to tell you that."

"I thought he'd just died natural. Dear God. Stabbed. Somebody trying to get his key?"

"I doubt it, because the key was still on him when the undertaker got him. Tied around his neck."

"I guess it wasn't Yates who killed him. No, couldn't have been. I got here before Yates did, and Spencer was already dead."

"Who's Yates?"

"A man who's after me. A man with one arm. I think you've met him."

"I have. What's his full name?"

"Yates. He's just Yates."

"Tell me this: was he the one who stole

your key on the *Sultana*?"

"The same."

"He's after the treasure?"

"After it like a crow after a flying bug. Who told you about how I lost the key?"

"Monty Wilks. It's kind of a legend around Memphis. So are you."

"I'm through with Memphis. I'm going to get my treasure at last. Because you've got the other key."

"Did you find your key, Joe?"

"Maybe I did, maybe I didn't."

"You needn't worry about telling me. I won't try to take it. It's rightfully yours."

"You got Spencer's key, though?"

"I did. At the moment it's out of my hands."

"What do you mean?"

"Before I answer that, can you tell me something? If I can help you get it back, will you let me talk to you some? Just about your family, your life, the things you did before Andersonville and after. It would help my book."

"I ain't much on talking."

"You could talk as much or as little as you want."

"Maybe I can do that. Where's the key?"

"In the custody of the city of Leadville. Namely, in the police station. Held for safekeeping by Marshal Martin Duggan."

"Damn!"

"Don't worry. It should be safe there."

"I can't go to no police station."

"Why?"

"I don't like police. And I'll be in trouble because of the grave."

"But you'd have both keys. You could get your treasure. That would be worth whatever little trouble the police would give you."

"I ain't going face-to-face with no town marshal, not here, not nowhere. Damn!"

It was the first obvious indicator I'd seen of the unstable nature of his mind. Twelve years of looking for his "key," finally finding it somehow, and now he was balking at completing his quest just because he didn't like policemen.

"How'd you find the key?" I asked him. "I'd have thought it was in the river, buried deep."

He looked at me with squinted eyes. "Don't know I want to tell just yet how I got my key."

"Why not?"

"I'll tell you only this: it wasn't in the river."

Intriguing. But I wasn't going to beg him for immediate information. Better to work things up slowly with this man, earn his trust. He'd open up soon enough. And the more he opened up, the stronger my book would be for it.

"What is the key, Joe? It has to be something written."

"It's what it is. My business and nobody else's. I can tell you this: if you had my part of the key, and my brother's part, and you sat and looked at them both, you'd not be an inch closer to finding that treasure than you would be if didn't have neither part."

"You speak in riddles, Joe."

He grinned, and it pulled me all the way back to the last time I'd spoken to this man, a time he'd grinned in exactly that same way. All the way back to that miserable prison camp where men died and maggots thrived. It made me shudder.

"I remember seeing your key when we were both prisoners, Joe. A piece of pipe, just like the one the undertaker took from your brother. But you'd never opened it, I don't think."

"Never had no chance to open it then. It was give to me just before the war. I carried it until I was captured, and managed to hide it. Know how I did that?"

"I heard."

"Clever, eh?"

"Not a place many would want to look for

something."

"That's right. Of course, there was no way to open it in the prison camp. No tools for sawing open a pipe."

"Then it was lost on the *Sultana* . . . until you found it."

"Until I found it."

"Have you opened it now?"

"Nope."

"Why not?"

"It was opened by somebody else."

"Who?"

"That's for me to know and you to forget about, because I ain't telling."

He stuck out his chin and grinned again. A big child, this man was. An overgrown but still undersized boy. But one who could draw pictures that pulled you into them and seemed to have a life of their own.

"So all that separates you from your treasure is getting that other key back from the marshal's office."

"That, and keeping away from Yates."

I played a hunch. "You said that key was never in the river. Know what I think, Joe? I think you never found that key at all. I think Yates never lost it. Lost his arm, but not the key. Maybe it was in his pocket. And he's had it all these years, and it's been useless to him because it's only part of the information. Or maybe it's in code. Anyway, I'm betting that you got that key back from Yates somehow. That's how you 'found' it. And he's not too happy about it."

McCade glared at me. Here was a man who should avoid poker, because his looks told me that I'd hit the truth or something very close to it. "I ain't saying nothing about all that," he said, sounding petulant.

"He's a dangerous man, Joe. I know that first-hand. I watched him beat a footpad to death with his own wooden arm. It was the most brutal thing I've seen since Andersonville. Of course, he saved my life by what he did. That footpad was ready to slice me up when Yates came in and turned him into jelly."

"He's the devil," McCade said, so serious now that he sounded quite intelligent. "The very devil himself."

"Did he track you here, Joe?"

McCade nodded.

"I'm going to advise you to do something you won't want to do. But I'll go with you, if that will help. We'll go and talk to the marshal. Ask him to give you some protection until Yates is found. They're looking for him already because he beat that street robber to death. Ask him to put you in the jail, if you want. I spent the night there. It's not that bad. And you'd be safe."

It was the wrong thing for me to say. He backed away, eyes filling with fire. "I see what you're doing, damn you!" he said. "You're trying to get me locked away so you can try to get your hands on my key, and get Spencer's key, too . . . then you think you'll get that treasure for yourself!" He jumped forward and thrust his face up, chin jutting more than ever, and snarled his next words right into my face. "Well, it wouldn't do you no good, Mr. Jed Wells! Because you couldn't read a word of either one of them, no, sir! Because you don't know the secret! Ain't nobody in this world that knows the secret now but me! Nobody but me!"

He wheeled and stomped off; again I had the impression of an overgrown child.

I watched him vanish and shook my head. This was the most remarkable, downright bizarre meeting I'd had for a long time.

Now I stood watching him go out of sight. But I'd do nothing about it.

Another meeting awaited me, in Gambletown. I had to find Katrina Ashe.

14

When I rode out of the town limits of Leadville, I did so in direct violation of the
instructions of Marshal Martin Duggan. So
be it. Given what Margaret Rains had told
me about Katrina's situation, I'd have de-
fied an order of the President himself.

It came to me that Katrina's situation was
in some ways akin to that of Josephus Mc-
Cade. He had a dangerous follower on his
trail. So did she.

The trail seemed longer this time than
before. But the day was beautiful, the sky
brilliant blue and sparkling like the gold in
Josephus McCade's dreams of treasure. My
horse was strong and steady. As I rode I fell
into a comfortable, half-sleeping state, letting the motion of the horse gently rock me.

The sight of a wagon ahead broke me out
of my reverie. At first glimpse I thought it
was the wagon of the Strand Players, but
the illusion vanished with a second glance.

This wagon was much smaller, and painted a toothy white. It was tilted precariously, one wheel lying on its side, having come completely off the axle.

A man in dusty but decently made clothing stood beside the tilting wagon, hands on hips and head shaking. A jack lay on its side beside the wagon, revealing failed effort on his part before I arrived.

I rode up; he looked up at me, hand above his brows like a salute, squinting at me as I drew near.

"Howdy," I said.

"Good day, sir."

I dismounted and tied my horse to a sapling, then walked over to join him in inspecting the wagon. I glanced up at the words on the side. HORACE JORDAN AFFORDABLE DENTRISTRY.

"I'm hoping you're a wagonmaker who set out this morning in hopes of finding some poor soul in need of your merciful services," Jordan said.

"Afraid not," I replied. "But I've got a strong enough shoulder and I've worked on wagons a few times in my life. I'd say you and me together could get that wheel back on."

"If so, I'll pay you any price you ask . . . within reason," said Jordan. "Pull some teeth for you, no charge."

"My teeth are fine," I replied. "Come on. Let's give this jack another try."

It took more than an hour of hard effort, because the jack was faulty and gave way at very inconvenient and dangerous moments. But eventually we had the wheel back in place.

"I'd get that looked at by a real wagonmaker when you get to Leadville," I said. "That's where you're headed, I assume."

"It is. I've been making the rounds back and forth between Leadville and Gambletown for nearly a year now."

"Can a dentist make a living that way?"

"I've done it so far. No wealth, just a living . . . but I can't complain. Eventually I'll have enough saved to put up a building and settle in at one place."

"Which town?"

"Whichever one looks the most promising whenever I reach that point. Probably Leadville."

"Have you been in Gambletown?"

"Just left there."

"Was there another wagon there . . . a troupe of actors?"

He looked odd, and reddened, quickly looking away from me. "Uh . . . yes. There was."

"Still there today?"

"Yes."

"Pardon me, sir, but you seem, perhaps, troubled or something."

"I'm . . . uh . . . I'm ashamed of myself, really. I didn't expect your question and it brought out the shame."

"Shame?"

"Of course. Are you familiar with the kind of show these . . . actresses perform?"

"I've got a notion of it. I know they were run out of Leadville."

"Shameful! Shameful, sir." He paused. "And even more shameful is that I gave into the temptation to go watch it. And me a Baptist deacon!"

"Was it really that bad?"

"It was fully indecent. Oh, some of it was put off as accident . . . the garment that falls unexpectedly, the skirt that gets caught on the nail and pulled a little too far aside . . . but it was positively a display of lewdness, pure and simple. And the rumor is that those women are indecent in more ways than as stage performers."

"But they are still there."

"Yes. Sir, I do hope you'll stay clear of them. You look a decent man."

"I'm no Baptist deacon, but I do try to live rightly. Let me ask you something: was there one of the actresses who was golden-haired, perhaps freckles on her nose, blue eyes . . ."

"Ah, yes. I remember her." He paused. "Oh, certainly her, more than all the others. Beautiful. Not ashamed to show her beauty, either." He paused again and I watched his earlier repentance fade and die under the glare of lusty memory. "Quite a sight, I must say. Quite a sight. She looked like an angel and acted like the devil. The devil in a skirt that just wouldn't stay on."

Suddenly I wanted to hit him. My fist actually balled up as if of its own accord. But I didn't strike him. He was simply telling me the reality of the life Katrina lived.

Impossible to believe. I remembered her as a child, rambunctious, barefoot, acting more boy than girl. I didn't want to think of her otherwise.

"Good day to you, Mr. Jordan," I said. "I've got to move on."

"Thank you for your help. Let me pay you."

"Nonsense." I touched my hat and headed for my horse. He watched me mount and ride away, on toward Gambletown.

My nerves were on edge as I rode into the little mining community. Meeting Katrina would be the first contact I'd had in many long years with the family of my lost fiancée, and it dredged up many long-forgotten emotions and memories. From the edge of town I saw the wagon parked up the dirt street, people moving about it. There was Lord Clancy, in his turban, looking haughty and royal.

And over beside the wagon, chatting in a flirtatious manner with a grizzled miner, was the very image of the woman I had once planned to marry. The sight of her stopped me cold and took away my breath, and maybe even my heartbeat, for several moments.

I knew it was not Kathleen, only her younger sister, but for a few brief seconds I allowed myself the joyful fantasy of seeing her as my forever-gone love. In my mind for a moment I became a husband returning home to his wife at the end of a long day, eager to hold her and bask in her company. It was foolish, but I did it, and the moment was worth having.

It was broken when Katrina let out a loud, somewhat coarse laugh, leaned over, and whispered something in the miner's ear that made him smile but also turn red. What could be said to a rough old miner that would get that kind of reaction I could only guess, but didn't really want to.

She saw me at that moment, and her face changed almost instantly. She studied me closely, making sure I was who she thought because it had been such a long time, then her face twisted like a baby's and she began to cry. The miner looked puzzled and watched her run away and toward me. I dismounted and she reached me just after I did so, throwing her arms around me and ramming me so hard I stumbled back against my own horse.

"Oh, Jed, Jed, you've come! I knew you would come to protect me!"

"Hello, Katrina. Lord, but you've changed a lot since I saw you last!"

"Oh, Jed, you've not changed at all! Still the same big, strong man, still so confident and handsome . . . oh, I knew when Margaret told me that she'd met a man named Jed Wells that you'd been sent by heaven itself to protect me! Oh, thank God you've come! Praise be!"

She seemed unusually religious for a woman who made part of her living prancing around half-clothed in front of leering miners and the other half, I assumed, lying on her back.

It was unnerving to hold her, virtually a stranger. It was more unnerving yet because she looked so much like Kathleen. She'd changed dramatically from the child I'd once known.

I gently pushed her back, looked at her, smiled. "Katrina, I can't believe I'm actually seeing you. Can you get away for a little while? Maybe we can sit down together and have a meal, or coffee."

"Yes. I want to."

She put her arm in mine and pulled me close. We walked side by side toward the nearest café.

Katrina lifted the coffee cup to her lips and took a sip, but her hand trembled slightly and her eyes cut from side to side while she drank. It appeared a habitual act of the sort done by someone accustomed to being forever on the lookout.

She lowered the cup, and her eyes, and stared at the tabletop as she spoke. Her voice was softer now, even more like Kathleen's. Again I was unsettled. This all had too much of a dreamlike quality.

"I've heard of your success, Jed," she said. "I'm so proud of you for having written such an important book."

"I'm proud of it, too. I'm not glad I had the experiences that led to it, but I am glad

I was able to turn them into something of value."

"It surely has changed your life."

"It has. Some I meet love me for that book, some despise me. A lot depends on how they stood during the war."

"And it's probably made you, you know, much more well-off, too."

Her eyes remained locked on the tabletop. She took another sip of coffee, hand trembling again.

The comment was intended as a question. I wasn't inclined to answer.

She looked up at me after a moment. I stared back at her, and smiled slightly.

"I so wish Kathleen had lived to marry you," she said.

"So do I."

Her lip trembled and tears spilled out of her eyes. "Oh, Jed, I'm so despairing! I've become so vile . . . I've done so much wrong!"

"How did it happen, Katrina?"

"My father and mother are dead, you know."

"I knew your mother had died. I didn't know about your father. When?"

"Almost two years ago. A cancer."

"I'm so sorry."

"I was left alone . . . and penniless. He'd

181

taken to gambling, you know."

"No, I didn't." It was hard to believe. Rolly Ashe had been a highly moralistic man when I'd known him, not touching a drop of liquor, and shunning cards. "Satan's calling cards," he'd called them. "When did he begin to gamble?"

"After Mother died. It changed him so. He became hard to live with. All wrapped up inside himself, bitter at the world and heaven and whatever else there may be."

"I'm sorry to hear it."

She held her cup in both hands now and took one more sip, then cleared her throat, wiped a tear away, and looked at me. "You probably are wondering how bad the things I've done have been. If I've become . . ." She looked away. "I've done what you are thinking. I've become the kind of harlot you're thinking of."

"Well . . . I don't know what to say to that. I'm sorry it came to that. And I'm ready to help you get away from that kind of life."

Her eyes met mine again. "Oh, Jed, do you mean that?"

"Of course I do. You're Kathleen's sister. For that reason alone I'd help you."

Her tears came again. Yet I wasn't touched by them. There was something in all that that was . . . uncomfortable. Even false.

182

I forced out a smile. "Can I buy you a piece of cake, some pie?"

"I think I'd like nothing more than a good piece of bread with some jam. Any kind of jam."

"I'll see what I can do." I rose and headed for the kitchen door, through which the woman running the place had vanished a couple of minutes before. I found her, placed the order, then came back out.

Katrina was pouring something from a flask into her coffee. She quickly corked the flask and put it away, out of sight.

I wished I hadn't seen that. It was becoming slowly apparent that I was dealing with a troubled woman here.

She smiled at me as I sat down again. "You'll have your bread and jam in just a minute."

"Thank you." She drank from her now-fuller coffee cup. Did she think I couldn't smell the whiskey?

"Katrina, it's my understanding that there is a man following you."

She looked solemn. "Yes."

"And that he's dangerous."

"I think he is."

"Has he tried to hurt you?"

"He's tried to take me away. Kidnap me."

"Do you know his name?"

"No. No. I don't know his name or how he came to know me."

"He was in one of your audiences, probably."

"I suppose so. Jed, why do you look bruised?"

"I had a row with a man in Leadville. I'm all right."

"That's good."

"You have to stop the life you're living, Katrina. Stop it today, here and now."

"How? What can I do?"

"You can come with me. I'll take you back to Leadville and put you in a hotel. We'll use a false name. You can be safe."

"Why Leadville? Can't we go farther away?"

"We can. We will. But for now I need to stay there. I'm supposed to be there now, in fact. The local law has a great interest in me right now."

"You're in trouble?"

"I witnessed a murder. And there was another situation, not worth going into right here. I need to remain in Leadville awhile longer. And there's a personal reason, too. Something involving a man I knew back at Andersonville."

"He's in Leadville now?"

"That's right. Believing he's on the verge

of finding a great treasure."

Her eyes gleamed and she suddenly looked hungry.

"But soon, we'll go. I'll take you away," I went on.

"To where?"

"I don't know. We'll talk about that later."

"Does this man really have a treasure?"

"He says he does. But he's loco. He's been loco for years."

"So there's no treasure."

"Probably not."

She sipped her coffee again.

"Has Margaret Rains come back?"

"No. I'm concerned about her."

"It was because of her letter that I came here. She wrote to me."

"I know. Oh, Jed, when she came and told me she had met a man named Jed Wells, and how you'd fought off a bad man, I knew, just knew, that I'd see you, and that you'd help me."

I smiled. "Here I am."

"Have you seen Margaret?"

"I've seen her, but she's vanished."

"I hope she's all right."

"So do I. I'll try to find her when we get back to Leadville."

"When will we go?"

"As quickly as possible. How much do you

have to bring with you?"

"It's all in one carpetbag. It's all I own, Jed. And I have no money."

"I'll take care of that."

"I feel guilty, you spending money on me." It didn't sound convincing.

"Don't worry. I can afford it."

She looked hungry again when I said that. "I'm glad you've done well, Jed. I'm very proud of you."

"Thank you."

She looked out the window. That hungry look changed to one of dread. "Oh no."

I'd spotted him already: a tall man in a bowler hat. Muttonchop whiskers, a tattoo on the side of his neck, fire in his eyes. Heading toward the café.

"Who is he?" I asked.

"Pike Vaughn. He owns the traveling show."

"He knows you're leaving?"

"I think he's figured it out. Watch out for him; he's a harsh man."

"I can be harsh myself when need be."

I would not face him inside the restaurant. I rose and headed out the door. He paused when he saw me, glaring.

"You . . . do you have Katrina Ashe with you?"

"I do."

"Send her out here. She works for me."

"I think she just resigned."

"I don't know who you are, but you'd best step aside."

"She doesn't want to talk to you. She's leaving your employ, and your show. Don't make an argument about it, friend."

"Hell with you." He advanced as if to go past me. I drew back my fist, aimed it at his jaw, and knocked him to the ground.

He looked up at me with an expression of astonishment. A little trickle of blood came out of the left side of his mouth. "The hell!" he bellowed.

"Sorry to have to do that. But I mean it when I say she doesn't want to talk to you."

"She owes it to me to talk to me! I been good to that sorry —"

"Watch what you say. I have a good stout kick, and I swear I'll have you swallowing your own teeth if you get disrespectful."

Vaughn rose slowly, keeping a keen eye on me the whole while. "Let me tell you this: you get yourself involved with that . . . with Katrina Ashe, and you'll live to regret it. She's a rattler, with the rattles cut off. No warning, just a bite. Pure poison bite. You better be slow to believe what she tells you. She and Margaret both. Rattlers with the rattles cut off, both of them, and liars."

187

"Thank you for the warning. Now I'll give you one: you cause the slightest problem, show your face anywhere in my sight again, and I'll show you how poison a bite really can be."

I turned and motioned to Katrina, who watched through the window. She emerged, looking scared. Vaughn glared bitterly at her, but said not a word.

She went to the wagon, the rest of the troupe watching her, and came out with a shawl over her shoulders and a carpetbag in her hand. She hugged a couple of the women, then came to me. I took her hand and led her away.

She rode behind me, her arms around my waist, and looked back at the people and life she was leaving as we moved out of Gambletown.

A figure stepped onto the road ahead of me. Lord Clancy, still in his turban, had somehow worked his way around ahead of us. He stood in the midst of the road, staring at me.

I pulled the horse to a halt. "I'm going on past you," I said. "Don't cause us any trouble."

"I won't, sir," he said. He walked up to me and put his hand out. "Good work back there. You could not have found a more deserving man to treat in such a way."

I shook the hand. He nodded curtly, then turned his head slightly so that his turban hid much of his face from Katrina's angle of view. He mouthed a single word: "Beware," and at the same moment flicked his eyes in Katrina's direction. It was a fast move, so subtle I hardly caught it myself, and I'm certain Katrina missed it completely.

"Good day," he said. Looking back at Katrina, he touched his turban and tilted his head. Without a word he turned and walked back into Gambletown.

15

It was a stroke of luck: the room beside mine was now empty. I quickly rented it for Katrina, but for purposes of the ledger gave her the name Mary Malone.

I supposed she must be tremendously relieved to be under the care of someone protective, because she moved into her room with the excitement of a newly married princess being shown her castle. "Oh, Jed, thank you," she said, over and over. "I feel so safe here."

My room was empty; no sign was there that Margaret had returned to it in my absence. I expressed concern to Katrina.

"Don't worry too much about Margaret," she said. "She knows how to take care of herself."

Katrina settled into her room, packing her few possessions into the wardrobe and generally acting like someone anticipating a lengthy stay. I warned her to keep her door locked, to let in only me, and to keep a lookout through her window for any evidence of her follower outside. She'd described him as a tall, yellow-haired, ruddy-faced man with pale eyes. Sounded like someone who should stand out in a crowd, anyway.

Giving her one more warning, I took to the street, partly looking for McCade and partly just making myself visible in case the local police had begun looking for me for any reason and had come to suspect I'd left town.

"Well, well!" a familiar voice said as I walked along a Front Street boardwalk. "There's the man himself!"

I turned and nodded a hello to Hinds, who was leaning against a wall, cleaning his fingernails with a broken-off pocketknife blade. I meandered over and shook his hand.

"How you faring, Estepp?"

"I can't complain. I hear you've had an interesting time or two in our fair city in the last little spell."

"How would you know what kind of times I've had?"

"Oh, I've got friends in the department of police, believe it or not," he said. "There's an officer or two here who actually kind of likes this old boy. I've given them a piece of handy information from time to time. It greases the skids of life to do that every now and again, I've found." He raised one brow and tapped me on the chest lightly with an extended forefinger. "You need to watch yourself. Because they're watching you."

"Who?"

"Some of the police. Not so much Duggan as some of the underlings. They don't trust you and they don't like you."

"Why?"

"Some of it is that book you did, I think."

"Ah. Old rebels do find me offensive at times."

"Some of it is that you seem to wind up in the wrong places and the wrong company."

"I've had a couple of unfortunate circumstances along those lines here in Leadville."

"Where there's smoke . . . you know how people think. Hey, I did hear some of the details. I'm glad you're alive and kicking. I hear that Slick Davy isn't."

"Slick Davy was beaten to death by a man who apparently is named Yates, and who has one real arm and one wooden one. You seen anyone around like that?"

"I ain't. But if he's in Leadville, eventually I will."

"He's dangerous. Don't get close to him."

"I heard the story. You're lucky to be alive."

"I'm still aching in my shoulder joints and still showing the bruises and so on."

A policeman came by, trotting along in a great hurry. A moment later another went the same way.

"They're all stirred up today," Hinds said. "Something must have happened."

"In a town as fluid as this one, my guess is that something happens a lot."

I parted from him, slipping him a dollar as I did so. I'd given him money once before. Probably not a good thing to do in that he would certainly buy liquor with it, but it was useful to have a man such as Hinds watching my back. I would not forget how he'd warned me about Slick Davy.

Continuing my walk, I kept my eyes open for McCade, for Yates, for Margaret Rains, for any male stranger who looked tall and blond and ruddy. But I saw none of these.

I pondered the strange warning that Lord Clancy had given me regarding Katrina. He was a stranger to me, and I had no grounds to trust him, but that warning had a ring of serious authenticity about it. I would heed it. After all, the Katrina Ashe of today was much different from the little girl I'd known long ago. She lived a rough life; in some ways she'd probably seen a lot more than I'd seen, and my own road had not been a smooth one.

Another policeman came running by, turning a corner and going out of sight. I followed him, and around the corner saw him making a left onto the next street, so in a hurry that he was nearly run over by a wagon.

Curiosity almost made me go after him, but I didn't do it. I'd already had adventures enough in this town without embroiling myself in situations that didn't involve me.

I continued my walk, then headed for a restaurant, where I ordered a good meal and had it packed on a tray. Making arrangements for the dishes to be picked up later, I carried the food to the hotel, and presented Katrina Ashe with one of the best meals she'd probably been offered for a long time.

As she ate joyfully, safe in a hotel room, enjoying company and food and an existence no doubt far removed from what she was accustomed to as part of a traveling troupe of actors, she seemed for the first time something like the Katrina I'd known. A girlish quality showed itself through her hardened veneer, and I put aside suspicions and warnings, and enjoyed the company of one who reminded me of happier days before war and imprisonment and loneliness.

We ate and talked about the past. It was a good moment, and I enjoyed it as much as she did.

And at the same time I ached deep inside, missing Kathleen more badly than I had in years.

I knew I was dreaming, but it was a vivid dream indeed, feeling quite real. I was in a crowded forest, dark and looming trees all around, all around me black, except for the treetops, which flared in brilliant flame. I struggled for air, my nostrils full of the stench of smoke . . .

Opening my eyes, I sat up. The covers were twisted tightly around me, constricting. The air was thick, full of smoke.

I freed myself from the covers, coughing, eyes burning. The smoke was not yet heavy, but it was pervasive, and thickening. I threw on my clothes and went to the door.

It was cool, so I opened it slowly, and looked out. Across the hall the door opened and another man also peered out, his white hair a tangled mess, his eyes bleary from sleep. Down the hall a woman, wearing a thick robe, emerged.

"Where's the fire?" the man across the hall asked.

"I don't know . . . the smoke is coming from downstairs, I think," I replied.

Katrina's door was still closed. I went to it and hammered on it. "Katrina! Wake up!"

I heard her move, then begin to cough. A minute later the door opened. She came out, blanket wrapped around her.

"Let's get out of here," I said. "This place may be about to go up."

I thought of my rifle, locked in the wardrobe, and my other possessions. But no. I would not get them. Get out of a burning building fast, I'd always been told. If you linger to collect what you think you must have, you die.

"Let's move on down," I said to her and the others around me. All the doors of occupied rooms were now open, the sleepy-eyed, nervous residents emerging in various states of half-dress. "Let's get onto the street. Listen! I hear the fire bell clanging. Let's move out quickly but carefully."

We moved as a group toward the stairs.

I'd anticipated flames, flickering light, crackling wood. But I saw none of it. Only a crowd of evicted, sleepy hotel residents clumped in the street, firemen moving

196

around and in and out of the building, policemen here and there, making sure everyone remained orderly.

"It started back in the office," said a resident from the ground floor. He was one of those types who spoke in a perpetually authoritative tone. "A cigar in a rubbish tin. It caught afire and lit a curtain. More smoke and smoldering than fire."

"Enough smoke it about filled up the upper floor," another man said. "There's got to be a good fire burning there somewhere."

The other shook his head firmly. "Nope. You'll get a lot more smoke from a smoldering fire than an open flame. This one's a smolderer. No question about it."

The evening had turned cold. Katrina huddled under her blanket, shivering, standing close to me. I found nothing to complain about in that.

"I'll be!" I said, looking to our left. "There's Josephus McCade!"

He was there all right, leaning up against the wall of the hardware store next door, watching the action. He hadn't noticed me, I didn't think.

"Is that the man with the treasure?" Katrina asked, very awake now.

"That's the man who believes he has a treasure. Somewhere. Though if he really

197

did, I think by now he'd have managed to have it."

"He's little."

"Not much to him, that's right. And his mind . . . something not quite right there. Hey . . . look at that. He's got the interest of the local constabulary all at once."

A policeman in the standard dark uniform of Leadville approached McCade, who reacted with surprising intensity when he saw him. McCade's mouth drew back in a semblance of a smile, but it was ghastly and unpleasant to see, like a face buffeted by a wind that was far too strong.

The policeman began talking to McCade in a hectoring manner, moving his hands around and glaring. McCade just kept giving him back that ugly, distorted smile of fear.

"Excuse me," I said to Katrina.

I moved a little closer, getting into better earshot of the harping policeman.

". . . and it's defacement, sir, pure defacement, and of a church, no less! What would lead you to do such a defacing thing? You tell me that!"

"It wasn't me."

"Ha! I know it was you, sir. I know who you are, and I know you draw pictures. And I spoke to a man who watched you do it!

So don't deny it was you!"

"Are you going to arrest me?"

"I might, sir, I might. Or I might offer you the chance to recompense for the defacement."

"To what?" McCade looked and sounded weak, like his strength was fading in the mere presence of a stern law officer. I noticed how he clutched the corner of the building, and thought how he looked very unstable and insane indeed at that moment.

"To make it right again. You take yourself a bucket and water, and you scrub that church wall clean, and I'll forget all about it."

The trembling McCade's lip quivered, then he brought out a question with great effort. "If I do, would you get something for me that's at the police station?"

"What's that, sir?"

"It's a short piece of closed-up pipe, hanging from a string."

"What?"

McCade said it again. "It's mine," he added. "The marshal is holding it for me."

"Then you must talk to the marshal about it. I know nothing of it."

"I don't talk to marshals."

"Then you don't get your pipe back. Merciful Mary, my friend, why do you want such a foolish thing as that, anyway? Listen to me: you worry about cleaning off that church wall, and forget other foolishness."

The policeman was called away then by another, who came out of the hotel coughing. They conferred a moment. The one who had been lecturing at McCade cleared his throat and said, "You may now return to the hotel. The fire is out and you will be safe. There is, unfortunately, a heavy smell of smoke you will have to endure."

Groans and murmurs from the crowd. They shifted forward. I motioned for Katrina to go on in with the others, and gave her a little smile and wave that in essence said, Good night. I'll not be talking to you further tonight.

She didn't take the hint. I watched her enter, then step to the side and wait for me inside the lobby.

I walked up to McCade. He sucked in his breath sharply when I said hello, as if I'd just jerked him physically and awakened him.

"Jed Wells," he said. "It's you, Jed Wells."

"And it's you, Joe McCade. What are you doing out roaming the town this time of night?"

"I like to roam at night."

"How are you?"

"Still waiting to get back my key, that's how I am. And that damned policeman wouldn't help me. He said I had to go to the marshal."

"Why don't you? You may have some trouble over having dug in your brother's grave, but I doubt the police really care much about that. If they had, that policeman just now would have hauled you in. The marshal isn't hard to talk to. You should do it."

"I don't talk to marshals."

"What about your treasure? Your key?"

"I don't talk to marshals. You can go get it for me. I ain't going."

"I'll help you get it, but they won't give it to me alone, because they know it's not mine. You'd have to be there."

"I despise police and jails and such. They scare me."

"I'd like the chance to interview you, Joe. To help my book be a better book. Will you let me talk to you sometime soon? If you will, you and I can go together and I'll get your 'key' for you. You don't have to come in, just stand out where they can see you and know that I'm not trying to take it for myself."

He pursed his lips, thinking, then said, "I'll talk to you. Maybe we'll do that."

"Good. I'll come see you after daybreak. Where will you be?"

"I been sleeping in a shed over near the graveyard. There's a clapboard house, a little barn painted kind of rusty red, and a shed out behind the barn. That's where I sleep."

"Are you safe enough there? Is Yates still around?"

"I ain't seen him. But he's still around."

"How do you know? Maybe he moved on, knowing the law was on the lookout for him."

"Yates ain't the kind to move on."

"What was that policeman harping at you about?"

"I drawed a picture on a wall. It was a church wall, and he says I shouldn't have drawed on a church."

"What did you draw?"

"A woman. A beautiful woman who I'm going to marry. I love her."

"I didn't know you had a woman."

"I just met her, here in town."

"Best wishes to you, then. I'll see you sometime in the middle of the morning. I'll bring you breakfast, how's that?"

"That's fine. Eggs and biscuits."

"Eggs and biscuits it will be."

16

Katrina was still waiting inside, wrapped up in her blanket.

"Did he talk about his treasure?"

"Not really. There's probably no treasure, Katrina. He's just a crazy old fellow who's too scared even to go talk to a town marshal. If there really was a treasure, I don't think something like that would stop him."

"I wonder what kind of treasure it is? Cash? Jewels?"

"Pure imagination, probably. Lord, it smells smoky in here! It'll be hard to sleep with that smell."

We went back up stairs, to our rooms. I opened the windows, pulled an extra blanket from atop the wardrobe and spread it on the bed, and lay down to get what little sleep I could for the rest of the night. The stench of the smoke made it hard to rest, and I sneezed several times. Katrina, in the next room, apparently was too awake to go back to sleep now. I could hear her moving around, doing things.

But finally I did sleep, and awakened with sunlight coming through the open windows. A cool breeze, too. I closed the windows, washed up, and went around to rouse Katrina. She was already awake and dressed.

"Want some breakfast?" I asked. "We could go together to a café, or I could bring it to you if you don't want to risk being seen by your follower."

"Do you think he's here, Jed? I haven't seen him. Maybe he's gone."

"How long has he been following you?"

"I've seen him in the last eight or nine towns we visited."

"Including Gambletown?"

"Yes . . . and here in Leadville just before that."

"Then he's still around. He doesn't sound like the giving-up type. But he may not know you're back in Leadville. He probably has no notion that you left the troupe and thinks you're still in Gambletown. Where is the troupe going next?"

"I don't really know. Through the mining country, that's all I know. All the towns seem the same after a while, and it doesn't matter where you are."

"We'll find a way to get rid of him, Katrina."

She smiled. "I'm tired of being cooped up here, Jed. I'll go with you to breakfast. I think surely it will be safe enough . . . I feel very safe whenever I'm with you."

"Put on your shawl and let's go."

We dined in a corner café, eating hot food and drinking hotter coffee. The day was clear and beautiful, the air fresh even though we were in busy, chimney-rich Leadville, and seeming even fresher yet in contrast to the smoky night just completed.

"I don't think we'll be lingering long here now," I said. "I'm going to talk to Josephus McCade this morning. I'm taking him breakfast, in fact. After that, I suppose there's no reason not to move on. We'll get you away from these parts, let your trail go cold, and find you something somewhere else, a way you can make a living without attracting attention. Especially the wrong kind."

"I don't know what I can do, Jed. I only know acting, and . . . the other."

"There's plenty you can do. You're young and smart and I'm sure very talented."

"If I was, I'd not have gotten myself into the situation I have." She looked out the window, wistful. "Oh, Jed, I like this town. I really do. I'm not in a hurry to leave it. Do we have to go so quickly?"

"What about the man following you? If we stay around here he's eventually going to find you, don't you think?"

"Maybe he's gone. Let's not leave here yet, Jed. Maybe I can find something I can do here. Maybe I can make a new life here . . . maybe you can, too."

The odd thing is, at that moment it actually sounded appealing. And she seemed more than appealing, more than ever like Kathleen come back to life, and not at all like a small-time prostitute and actress whose skill consisted of "accidentally" losing her bodice while spouting garbled Shakespeare. So I sipped my coffee and nibbled at my eggs and let myself think about it, and not rule it out.

I was a writer. I could live anywhere. Right now I had no real home, just a few rented rooms in Denver that I visited a few times in a year. The rest of my time I stayed on the move, visiting the kin of those I'd known at Andersonville, and collecting experiences for my writing.

It wasn't a bad life, but it was lonely, unstable, and without a sense of home. What if I changed that? Would it be a bad thing?

"Let's worry about that later," I said. "For the moment, we're here. I've got a man I need to interview, and the local law wants me to remain about, anyway. I don't think I'm under any real obligation to do so, but if you want to stay awhile, we can stay."

"Good, Jed," she said, reaching across the table and patting my hand.

It didn't make a lot of sense, really, her wanting to remain hereabouts while she was supposedly being followed by a man grown obsessed with her. But her presence was like the aroma of a heady perfume, distorting things, standing common sense on its head.

I realized how long it had been since I'd enjoyed the company of a woman in this way. It made me feel younger and — odd as it sounds, given what her way of life had been — cleaner, less soiled by the world.

I realized that the last time I'd felt this way was before the war, before my days of dealing death with my sharpshooting rifle, before Andersonville and all the ugliness there.

We talked some more, about nothing important. The sun grew brighter outside. I ordered another breakfast and had it packed up on a covered tray, promising to pick it up in a few minutes.

I escorted Katrina back to the hotel and

to her room. She gave me a kiss on the cheek as I turned to go, and I felt the warm tingle of it for minutes thereafter.

Watch yourself, Jed Wells, I said to myself. *Don't let this woman make you lose your head.*

But really, the prospect of losing my head didn't sound too bad. I was a lonelier man than I'd realized.

Bearing the breakfast-laden tray across town, I headed for the vicinity of the cemetery and saw Baudy Wash heading across the street, carrying a sloshing bucket and an armload of rags.

"Baudy!" I called. "Good morning!"

He stopped and squinted in my direction, then nodded. "Good morning, sir." He eyed the tray. "You going to eat breakfast somewhere, I see."

"It's for somebody else, actually. How are you doing?"

"I'm fine, sir. Going over here to wash a picture off a church wall."

"Oh, I think I know what you're talking about. I heard a policeman talking about it last night."

"Yes, sir. Picture of a woman on the wall of a church. It ain't a bad picture, but the church preacher don't much like it because . . ." He lowered his volume and glanced about before continuing. ". . .

because she's knowed to be a whore, sir, this particular woman."

"Where's the picture?"

"Yonder." He pointed north. A small white church stood there, half a block away, with a wooden cross on the front crest of the roof. I walked over toward it with Baudy.

"I know that woman," I said, looking at the image of Margaret Rains charcoaled onto the church wall in the distinctive style of Josephus McCade. It was not an indecent picture in any way, simply a portrait of her attractive face, with hair billowing around. *Some of Josephus's best work,* I thought. It was too bad it was destined for such a short life. I wished I had a photographer at hand.

Josephus had said he was in love. I had to chuckle. Half-crazy, homeless, penniless, dirty, and in love. With a traveling actress and prostitute who knew how to act classy but whose life was probably as low and vulgar as a life can be. What a pair!

But it made me feel sorry for Josephus. This was a love bound to go unrequited. I couldn't imagine Margaret Rains, or any other woman, ever falling in love with Josephus McCade. He'd probably scraped up some money to pay her for a tryst and had lost his lonely heart to her in the process.

"Did the preacher hire you to wash this off?"

"Yes, sir."

"You know who drew this?"

"No, sir."

"Remember the man you saw digging in the grave?"

Baudy looked astonished. "He did this?"

"Yes. By the way, he's no ghost or resurrected corpse or any such thing. He's one of two twin brothers. One is buried in your graveyard. That's why the man you saw digging in the grave looks like the man buried in the grave."

"I'll be!"

"He was trying to find something he thought had been buried with his brother."

"Huh!"

"He's also the man I bought this breakfast for. He's an interesting man. Want to meet him?"

"Uh . . . no, sir. I don't believe I do."

"Have a pleasant day, Baudy."

"You too, sir."

Josephus was there, waiting for me. I was somewhat surprised. It was easy to find him. I looked for that small red barn, and there was indeed a shed behind it. Josephus was in back of it, seated on an empty crate, shaving with a razor that looked mighty dull to me. Cold water, too, and no soap. His looking glass was a piece of broken mirror.

"Good Lord, Joe, doesn't that hurt?" I asked him as I brought the tray around to him.

"A man's got to look his best when he's courting a woman."

"Your picture is being washed off the wall right now by the young fellow who digs graves at the cemetery. The preacher hired him to do it."

"Good. It means I don't have to mess with it." He dragged the dull razor across his whiskers and made a face of great pain as it shaved a few of them off, leaving behind as many as it got. "Did you bring what I asked?"

"I did."

He put aside the shaving for a spell and ate his breakfast with half his whiskers gone, the other half still there. It was a comical sight, but I didn't laugh. I didn't know Josephus McCade well enough to know how he'd take being laughed at.

When he was finished, he sighed loudly in satisfaction, wet his whiskers again, and went back to shaving.

"I don't know that I like you writing me

up in a book without me knowing about it," he said.

"It isn't really you, Joe. It's a completely fictional fellow I've named Garner. He's not you. He's just a made-up person who was inspired by you. Do you see the difference?"

"I don't know. Maybe. Hey, what did you think of my picture on the church? Pretty, ain't she!"

"She is pretty. A beautiful woman."

"I'm going to marry that woman."

"Joe, no offense, but do you really think a woman like her and a man like you could ever really be a married couple?"

"Why not? I'll have my money soon enough. I'll be able to take care of her. You're going to help me get back poor old Spencer's key, and once I've got that, I'll know exactly where to find that treasure."

"Do have even a notion of where it is, or what it is?"

"I know exactly what it is. And I could probably get in ten miles of it right now, without knowing a thing beyond what I know now."

"Can I take some notes while I talk to you?"

He thought about it, then shook his head. "No. No. I tend to trust you, Jed Wells. I thought you were one of the better ones back when we were in prison camp. But you might just be after my treasure."

"I've already made treasure enough for myself through my writing. I'm not wealthy by some standards, but for a single man with few expenses, I'm sufficiently well off. I vow to you, I don't want your treasure. Just to know more about you."

"Take your notes, then. But if I don't like your questions, I may not answer." He squinted at his scraggly, stubbly face in the mirror, and took another painful swipe with the razor.

I could tell he was enjoying the attention, but trying to be blasé about it.

"Tell me where you come from, Joe."

"North Carolina. There along the coast."

"Were you and Spencer the only children in your family?"

"The only boys. We had one sister. She died when she was twelve. Got sick and died a week later. My poor old mother got sick herself a month after that, and died too."

"What about your father?"

"He was a drunk. He tried to be a good man, but he couldn't. His brother was better. He raised me and Spencer more than Pa ever did. He died right about the time the war began."

"What was his name?"

"Clooner McCade. Spent years at sea, then settled down and ran a little general store. What time he wasn't poking around up and down the coast, exploring caves and such. He loved the sea and the coast, Uncle Clooner did." He paused and looked at me. "He found a lot of interesting things over the years."

"Ah. Including some things of value, maybe?"

"North Carolina had plenty of pirates along its coasts for a lot of years, you know."

"I've heard that." I thought things over a few moments. "It was your uncle who gave you the keys, wasn't it."

He looked at me from the corner of his eye, then back at his jagged-edged looking glass.

"He was a good man, Clooner was. But he cared little for money and such. We'd always thought he'd found things in those caves and such that he never told about. I think he was glad just to let it sit where it was, and draw from it from time to time as he needed money. He never made much of a living in that little store of his. We never could figure out how he survived." McCade swirled his razor in the water. "Every now and again he'd vanish for a few days, then come back, and all at once he was set up

214

with money again."

"He was selling off pieces of a treasure he'd found?"

"Me and Spencer always suspected so. So did Clooner's son."

"He had a son."

"Not proper like, he didn't. Fathered him with a whore girl who died when the boy was born. Clooner raised him, but he went wild as a buck before he was even full growed. Never was nothing but a source of grief to his father, that boy was. That's one reason Clooner took so good to me and Spencer. We were better boys. More like sons to him than his own son ever was."

"What was his son's name?"

McCade lowered the razor and looked at me for several seconds, seemingly debating about whether to answer.

"His name is Yates," he said.

17

When I grasped what he'd just said, it brought me to my feet. My notepad fell to the ground, where it lay ignored.

"Wait a minute, Joe . . . the man with one arm . . ."

"That's my cousin. That's Yates McCade."

"He was on the *Sultana* with you?"

"He was. He was a prisoner of war just like us."

"He was in Andersonville?"

"No. The Cahaba prison. There were quite a few from there on the *Sultana,* along with those of us from Andersonville."

"This intrigues me, Josephus. How is it that Clooner gave the key to his treasure to his nephews instead of his own son?"

"I already explained that. We were more sons to him than his own son was. Yates has been trouble from when he was young. He's a thief, and worse. Much worse."

I remembered the cold viciousness with

which he'd beaten Slick Davy to death while I watched. The man he'd killed had been as wicked as they come, but still it had been a terrible thing to see.

"Why did he create the two 'keys,' and divide them between you?"

McCade made his final pass with the razor, then washed off his face. He was still rough and ragged, but he had made some improvement.

"At the time the war broke out, Spencer and I argued. Not about the war, but about a woman. We came to hate one another, we did, and it broke Uncle Clooner's heart to see it. Spencer and I both left for war on the same day . . . and the morning of that day, Clooner gave us the keys, already sealed up in their pipes. 'You two have the chance for a great treasure now,' he told us. 'But only together,' he says. 'Neither of you will find it unless you put your two keys together.' It was his way of trying to make us come back together and be friendly again, you see."

"But it didn't happen."

"No. The time it all came about made it so we couldn't get back together even if we'd wanted. The war took us both to different places, each of us bearing his key with him."

"And when the war was done, there was the *Sultana* incident, and you wound up on your island, searching for your key for years . . ."

"Yes, while Spencer went off all across the country, doing this job and that. Mostly trying to be a miner. We were stubborn, both of us. Full of pride. That was part of it. And there was also the fact that Spencer didn't have any notion about where I was. A man's hard to find when he's living alone on an island in the river."

"Yates knew about the treasure, and the keys?"

"Yes. And he despised his father for having passed him by. That's why he killed him."

"Yates murdered his own father?"

"After we went off to war, he got wind somehow that his father had found a treasure. He tried to make his father tell him where it was, but Clooner wouldn't. He told him that he'd decided that treasure was to go to me and Spencer, that Yates didn't deserve it. Yates flew off the handle and hit him. Too hard. He took off after that, fled out into the war before they even had Clooner in the ground."

"How did you know about it?"

"I didn't, for a year or so after it happened. My father sent a letter to me, and I guess one to Spencer, too. He begged us to get back together, 'for poor Clooner's sake,' as he wrote it. Pshaw! He wanted a share of the treasure, you see. But he died right after he sent that letter. Drunk himself to death."

I laid it all out to make sure I understood. "So at that point you and Spencer were out, fighting in the war but not together. You each had half a map, or guide, or whatever it is, telling you how to find this treasure. But neither of you alone could find it."

"That's right."

"And Yates was out there, too, knowing about the treasure and the two keys. But he didn't know where you were, and was busy as a soldier himself."

"You've got it right, Jed Wells."

I went on. "Late in the war you're taken prisoner. You manage to keep your key with you even through Andersonville. Then the war ends, you're set free, and you wind up on the *Sultana,* heading up the Mississippi. But what you don't know is that Yates has also been freed from a prison camp and is on the same boat."

"When I saw him on that boat, I almost keeled over in a faint. There was murder in his eyes. We were packed together like fish in a salt barrel on that boat, but he worked

219

his way over to me. Struggled with me, got the key out of my pocket. Then shoved me over the side and into the river. He laughed and mocked and waved that bit of pipe in the air . . . and shortly after that, the boilers blew."

"And Yates lost an arm, and the key."

McCade simply looked at me, cocking up one brow.

"Wait," I said, thinking a little more deeply. "You told me that when you got the key back, it wasn't because you found it by the river. You got it back some other way."

He smiled, just a little.

"Yates never lost the key, did he!"

"I think I've said all I need to about that."

"No, tell me if I'm right: you got the key back from Yates himself," I speculated. "What happened? Did he track you down on your island? You did become something of a legend . . . people knew your story. Yates may have heard it, too, and known it was you."

McCade clearly enjoyed watching me trying to piece together a puzzle that he already knew the solution to. He had nothing to say.

A new thought came to me. "If he still had the key, why would he need to find you? It would be Spencer he needed to find."

"Maybe he had the key, but needed a little

help in reading what was written on it."

"But he'd opened it . . . could he not read it?"

"Not the way Clooner had wrote it out."

"But *you* could read it."

McCade nodded. "Me and Spencer and Clooner, we were the only living people in this world who could read what was wrote on the papers Clooner had sealed up into those two pipes."

"A code."

"Not a code. Not to us, anyway. Maybe to you and everybody else in the world, but not to us."

"Please, Joe, explain this."

"I've said all I wish to say about that."

"I want to understand."

He paused, looking at me. "Don't know why I'm so inclined to talk to you, sir. Something about you makes me want to tell you things."

"It's a trait I have. I noticed it in Andersonville. People would tell me things they wanted passed on to their families if they didn't survive and I did. I don't know why that is, but it's a fact."

"All right, let me tell you how them letters was wrote. Twins growing up together like me and Spencer did sometimes come up with special ways of talking to each other when they're young. You ever heard of that?"

"Private languages. Yes, I've heard of that."

"That was us. We came up with a way of talking that would be gibberish to anybody else, but we understood it. A full language, all our own. Uncle Clooner thought it was the most interesting thing he'd ever heard. So we taught him how to talk it, too. The three of us, and our own language. You couldn't have had a better code."

This was fascinating. I'd already mentally scrapped the entire first draft of my book. This story was better than anything I could dream up on my own for my McCade-based character.

"Tell me about Spencer. When did he start writing you letters on the island?"

"Couple of years ago. He'd heard tales about somebody living on an island in the river, looking for a lost key. He didn't know it was me for a good while, then somewhere along the way he heard the name folks had come to call the island, and figured out it was me. I started getting letters from him, postmarked Leadville. He'd mail them to the postmaster in Memphis, and he'd have them sent over to me when folks brought supplies."

"Did you write him back?"

"I wrote him back after the first letter and

told him not to write to me anymore. I was still bitter at him over the woman, even though she was long gone. Dead, in fact. She'd married another man, died giving birth to a daughter. I still despised Spencer because of her. But Spencer kept on writing to me anyway."

"You used his letters for drawing paper."

"Paper is hard to come by on an island. I've always drawed my pictures on anything I could find."

"So at first you rejected Spencer's attempts to pull you two back together. But obviously you changed your mind, otherwise you'd not be here in Leadville right now."

"I did change my mind."

"Because you had gotten your lost key back."

He grinned again. "That would give a man good reason to want to be friends with his no-count brother again, now, wouldn't it?"

"You must have run across Yates. Somehow gotten the key from him."

"I'd always assumed it was lost in the river when the *Sultana* went down. I found out I was wrong."

"So somehow you got your key back from Yates, came to Leadville, and found that Spencer was dead."

"That's right. Dead and buried in a

pauper's grave, and I had no notion where that key could be unless it was buried with him."

"So you tried to dig him up. Got the job partly done one time, got run off when the graveyard tender showed up, then came back later and this time got the job done. But you found no key, as we both know."

At this point, Josephus McCade grew quite serious, and that odd look he had, the one that spoke of a mind not quite right, actually went away completely and he seemed as normal a man as I'd ever known. "I wish I'd never dug him up. I wish I could have seen his face while he was still a living man, not a man dead and decaying in his grave." He stared off past me, shuddered a little, and the moment passed. "If I'd been thinking better, I'd have thought his possessions might have been took by the undertaker. I'd have looked there first, instead of in his grave."

"Go back to Yates for a minute. He must have come looking for you on your island, to get you to translate the key for him."

"He did come to the island. He'd heard those Memphis legends about the crazy man on the river island, and figured out it was me, just like Spencer had. He appeared one day, wooden arm in place of the one the *Sultana* had blowed off. He had guns, knives . . . and the key. Not the pipe, that was long gone. He had only the paper that had been in it. But he couldn't read it, of course."

"Did you translate it for him?"

"No. I held firm. He tied me up, beat me, burned me . . . I've still got the burn marks on my back. But a one-armed man don't do a good job of tying knots. I worked loose of my ropes, and managed to clout the bastard in the head. Knocked him cold. I hit him two more times, trying to kill him, then dumped his sorry hide in the river. Then I sat down and read what Uncle Clooner had wrote down for me. Finally got to read it. All that long time after he'd give it to me, I'd finally got to read it. The funny thing is, it wouldn't have helped Yates to know what the key said. It only told half the story of where to find the treasure. You have to have Spencer's part to complete the story."

"He survived what you did to him, and followed you to Leadville."

"I don't think he followed me as such. I think he got back to the island somehow and read some of Spencer's letters, like you did, and figured out that Leadville is where I would go."

"Where is the key now, Joe?"

He gave me a triumphant look, and tapped the side of his head.

"You memorized it?"

"I know it like a baby knows the face of its mother."

"And destroyed the original?"

"Burned it to ashes, right there on the island. Then I headed off for Leadville to find Spencer. Thinking, of course, that Yates was dead. But it's like they say: it's hard to kill the devil."

"Joe, do you think it was Yates who killed Spencer?"

"No. Yates would have taken Spencer's key."

"So who did kill him?"

"This is a town where merchants walk home at night carrying a pistol in their hands in case a footpad jumps them. This is a town where you can build a shed on a lot to claim it, and have a whole gang of lot jumpers run you out of it, tear it down, and build their own to make it theirs. I watched that very thing happen the day I arrived in this town. Spencer could have been killed by anybody in a town like this."

"You realize, Joe, that once you get back Spencer's key, you'll be in more danger than ever from Yates."

McCade shrugged. "Nothing I can do about that."

"Maybe Yates is gone, Joe. Maybe, with me having witnessed him commit a murder, he's too afraid of the law to have stayed around here."

"I don't believe it. Two times that man should have been gone, two times he's not. I'll be rid of him when he's lying in his grave or I'm lying in mine, not before."

"Then be careful."

He stood. "I want it, Jed Wells. Let's go get my key."

"If we can. They may not let me get it without your permission."

"You've got my permission. I ain't going in no marshal's office."

"Why are you so afraid of the law?"

"There was a policeman in Memphis who heard all the stories about me and from time to time would come over and arrest me on one false charge or another. He'd haul me back across the river and throw me in the jail, and he'd torment and hurt me, trying to get me to talk. It never worked, but I've got no use for law now. No trust of them at all. I see a uniform and it makes something run through me like I can't even explain. I nigh piss my pants sometimes."

"You can wait outside the police station. I'll see what I can do."

18

As he had told me his history, Josephus McCade had seemed quite a sensible and sane man, for the most part. But as we walked toward the police headquarters and jail, he became wild-eyed and hard-breathing, that obsessive fear of policemen overtaking him and reminding me that he was, indeed, not a normal human being.

"I see the marshal's horse, right there," he said, pointing toward a nearby hitchpost. "He's in there. You go tell him that Josephus McCade wants his brother's possessions. You tell him that for me."

"Tell him yourself," I suggested. "There he is. Put that fear of yours behind you and just talk to the man."

Duggan had just emerged from a café just behind us, picking his teeth with a matchstick. He paused when he saw us, and studied us closely. He advanced, and McCade sucked in his breath and literally cringed . . . and Duggan was not even wearing a uniform.

"Gentlemen," he said, studying McCade closely. "Pretty day."

"Hello, Marshal," I said.

"You, sir," he said to my companion. "Are you McCade?"

McCade nodded, eyes wide and glaring at the marshal.

"Why are you so nervous, McCade? You got some reason to be nervous around me? What have you done?"

McCade said nothing.

"Maybe you're concerned about our local regulations regarding not digging up graves. But if you are, you can quit worrying about it. I checked, and it winds up we've never gotten around to making any laws about that in this town, nor county. I haven't bothered to check at the state level and ain't inclined to. I'm more inclined to forget about it — if you don't do it again."

McCade nodded rapidly.

"We'll forget about the grave incident . . . but I remain concerned with other things I'm beginning to hear about you, McCade. I hear some folks, women in particular, think you're a frightening man. They believe you're a likely footpad or blackleg of some other variety."

"I ain't, I ain't," McCade croaked out. He was sweating visibly and, oddly, seemed to struggle for air.

"A man lives in the streets and sleeps in sheds, he can make folks ill at ease. He can make the local law ill at ease, too. If I keep hearing folks complaining about you, I might have to give you lodgings in my jail there, until we can find something better to do with you." He chewed on the toothpick as McCade turned white as a bride's petticoat. "Or maybe you could just find another town to live in. That would lessen our interest in you completely."

"Marshal, Mr. McCade might indeed move on, but there is something keeping him here at the moment. He has asked me to make a request of you regarding that," I said. "He'd like to claim his late brother's personal items, in particular the little piece of pipe on a string that you're holding."

"That right, McCade?"

McCade nodded.

"Easy enough. Just step inside and fill out a paper for me."

McCade's breath whistled in sharply between his yellowed teeth. "I can't go in there. I go in there, and I can't breathe."

The marshal laughed. "We got air in there just like everywhere else."

But even now McCade was gasping. His lungs wheezed loudly. He backed away, shaking his head, chest straining.

"Are you all right, man?" Duggan said.

McCade turned and ran away.

"What the devil?" Duggan asked me.

"He's got a mortal fear of policemen and jails. Something going back to Memphis, where he used to be."

"Pitiful. I almost feel sorry for the old vagrant."

"What about his brother's items? May I claim them for him?"

"Can't really turn them over to you, sir. Not without his written permission."

"Then can I have the paper he needs to sign? I'll find him and get him to sign it."

"He'll have to sign it in the presence of an officer."

"I'll talk him into it. But in the meantime I hope you'll make sure that piece of pipe is secure in your office. There's a man in town besides McCade who would love to get hold of it."

"Why in the devil is that piece of rubbish so important?"

"You wouldn't believe it if I told you."

"Listen, you see McCade again, tell him I know about him drawing on that church wall. You tell him no more of that. He'll be gasping for air inside one of my cells if he does more of that. I'd have told him myself if he hadn't run off so fast."

"I'll tell him. Now, can I get a copy of that form he needs to sign?"

"Come on inside. I'll get you one."

Halfway back to the hotel, I saw a man who caused me to forget at once about Josephus McCade. He was tall, blond, very ruddy. He walked purposefully along a boardwalk on the far side of the street. Physically he matched exactly the description Katrina had given of the man following and terrorizing her, but his manner confused me. There was nothing covert or suspicious about the way he moved about. His height made him stand out, anyway, but in addition he had his chest thrust out, head and shoulders back, hat tilted up on his head. He whistled while he walked, and smiled and tipped his hat to passing people.

When the man turned and entered a gun shop, I headed across the street and entered after him, then pretended to look at a display of locally made leather holsters.

The man went to the counter and spoke to the clerk. I listened closely, and from his words and the clerk's responses surmised that he was not a known customer. Which probably meant he was not local, or not long local, anyway.

I watched him while pretending to be fascinated by the holsters. The clerk began bringing out various small pistols for examination.

Might this be Katrina's pursuer? If so, was there something ominous in his apparent impending purchase of a pistol? I left the store and hurried on to the hotel.

As I neared it, I looked up just in time to see a woman making a quick turn around a corner and going out of sight. It was Margaret Rains; I'd caught a clear look at her pretty and distinctly chiseled profile. And through the front door of the hotel I saw, in the shadows, the equally identifiable form of Katrina. She and Margaret obviously had been talking.

I wasn't certain, but I thought Katrina had seen me. Her shadowy form vanished.

When I entered the hotel, she was not in the lobby. I climbed the stairs. Her door was closed.

I knocked gently. No reply.

"Katrina?"

I heard a rustling on her bed.

"Katrina, are you there?"

"Just a minute." Her voice was heavy, as if with sleep.

The door opened and she smiled at me, eyes drooping, hair disheveled. "Hello, Jed. I'm sorry . . . I lay back down again and fell asleep."

She was lying. I'd seen her clearly in the lobby.

"I just wanted to make sure you were all right," I said. A pause, then: "I saw Margaret Rains going around the corner outside."

"Really? She was here?"

"Yes." Why did she not want me to know she'd been talking to Margaret Rains? Did they have some kind of scheme afoot?

I remembered the warnings I'd received from Katrina's old employer and from Lord Clancy.

"Did Margaret seem well? I wonder why she's not with the troupe?"

I had a strong suspicion that Katrina already knew. And I suspected that what she knew was that Margaret was stringing along foolish old Josephus McCade in case he really did have a cache of treasure somewhere, and Katrina was maybe in on it in some way herself. "Margaret seemed in a hurry. Josephus McCade is smitten with her, by the way. Pretty seriously."

"Oh? Did you meet him like you planned?"

"I did."

"Did he tell you about himself . . . his treasure and so on?"

"He told me a good deal."

She had her hungry look again; I didn't like it. "Is it true? Does he really have a treasure hidden somewhere?"

"He says he does. It could be true, I guess."

"Close to here?"

"A long way from here. All the way on the eastern coast."

"Oh. Well, I hope he is able to find it."

"He believes that with money, he'll be fit to have a woman like Margaret Rains. Sad, really. There's no way a man like Josephus could hope to have someone like her really love him. She might love his money, maybe, but not him."

"Oh, don't say that. I believe she could love him. But if he has money . . . all the better. What's wrong with money?"

I changed the subject. "Katrina, I saw a man in town . . . he looked like the man you described who is following you. I don't know if it was him."

"Tell me about him."

I told her all I'd seen.

"It's him. It's him. He's come after me."

"I'm concerned about the fact he was

buying a pistol."

"So am I. Jed, I'm scared."

"Then we'll make sure he doesn't see you. We'll get away from Leadville as soon as we can, and get you to someplace he'll never find you. I promise, Kathleen."

She tilted her head and looked at me quizzically. "Kathleen?"

"I'm sorry. I didn't mean to call you that. You just remind me of her sometimes. Quite a lot."

She smiled, reached up, touched my cheek. "That's nice."

Suddenly it was all very uncomfortable. Here was a young woman whose life had taken her down bad roads very early. A young woman who had just carried on a pretense regarding Margaret Rains. A young woman who'd been described to me as a snake with the rattles cut off.

I didn't want to believe such things about her. I ached for her to be like Kathleen . . . to *be* Kathleen.

I had not realized how much I missed my lost love.

"I . . . I'll let you lie back down and rest some more," I said. "I may go do some writing in my room."

She reached up, gave me a peck on the

cheek, and withdrew into her room, closing the door.

Night. Another Leadville day past, another mantle of darkness laid across the mountains and the broad terrain upon which the town stood.

I'd had supper brought to my room and hers, and we'd dined separately, me claiming not to feel well. The truth was, Katrina had me too turbulent inside to allow me to be with her. I didn't trust her . . . I didn't trust myself with her.

I wanted to draw her close, wanted to run away from her. All at the same time.

I retired early, and fell asleep quickly.

Her scream awakened me. I sat upright, wondering if I'd dreamed it. Something thumped hard against the wall, and she cried out again.

I was up and out the door in a moment. Clad only in longjohns, but not even conscious of that. Her door was closed, but the latch was broken. Someone had entered this room by force.

The same ruddy-faced man I had seen earlier was inside. He turned a face to me that was twisted with fury, lips pulled back against his teeth, eyes big and full of anger.

"Who the hell are you?" he said.

238

Katrina was on the floor, her gown torn, her hands over her face. She cringed like a terrified small animal.

I threw myself at him. My fist found his chin, his jaw. My other fist slammed his gut, and my knee came up and rammed his groin. He fell to the side with a loud grunt, then leaned over and heaved up the contents of his stomach.

Katrina made a faint, murmuring sound, her fists clenched so tightly that her nails and knuckles were paper white.

"Run, Katrina!" I said. "Get out and into my room, and lock the door!"

She did not move, too terrified. Her attacker was trying to rise, though, vomit on his chin, his arms flailing as he came up.

I kicked him in the kidney, driving him against the wall. The entire building seemed to shake as his big form slammed the plank wall, and I heard a man in the next room yell out, asking what the devil was going on.

Katrina looked at me pleadingly. I said, firmly, "Get up and into my room! Lock the door!"

This time she obeyed. She rose, clinging to her torn gown, and went out the door.

Her exit diverted just enough of my attention to give the ruddy-faced man an opportunity. He moved, rose again, and this time a small pistol was in his hand, apparently drawn from beneath his coat.

I saw it, and reacted reflexively, ducking away. He lifted the pistol and clicked back the hammer . . .

I rammed him with my shoulder. The pistol went up but did not fire. Somehow I managed to get hold of his wrist and twist it. He dropped the weapon.

Shoving me back with his greater weight, he abandoned his pistol and ran out the door and down the hall. I heard him thunder down the stairs.

Exiting the room myself, I almost ran after him. The man from the next room was coming out in the hall, frowning, looking ready to fight. "What's going on out here?" he demanded.

I ignored him, trying the knob on the door of my room. Katrina had been so distraught she had failed to lock it. I opened it and went in. She screamed, then when she saw it was me, rushed to me and threw her arms around me.

"Katrina," I said, "I had doubted you. I admit I was unsure there even was anyone chasing you. I thought you might have lied to me. I was wrong. I'm sorry. I'm sorry."

She held me and sobbed. I didn't blame her. The attack she had suffered had been terrifying, more violent in its way than even the death of Slick Davy.

"We need to get you out of here," I said to her. "Let's get everything packed and we'll go find another hotel. Come on, come on . . . it will be all right now. It will be all right."

A noise, in Katrina's room . . . then a shadow moved in the doorway, and I realized what a dreadful mistake I'd just made. I turned as the ruddy-faced man thrust his pistol into the doorway, aimed it at me, and fired.

19

The bullet clipped off part of my collar and slapped into the wall behind me. I roared in fury and lunged at him as Katrina threw herself behind the bed. He fired a second shot, but far too hurriedly. It missed me by a foot and shattered the window.

I cursed myself for a fool even as I got hold again of his gun hand and twisted. This time he didn't drop the pistol, though. I twisted harder, bones threatening to break. He dropped it now, but deftly, catching it in his other hand.

He struck me with it, then as I went down, tried to step over me, to reach Katrina. I pushed up, bumping him from below as he passed over me. He fell and lost his pistol, then grabbed it again.

The next seconds, or perhaps minutes, became a misery of violence, the details of which I would never recall with full clarity. I fought harder than I had fought in many a year, my fists aching from the impact, my own body suffering under his blows. In the end he ran from the room, pistol in his possession again. This time, I knew, he would not return.

Still only in my longjohns, I ran after him, down the stairs and through the lobby. He was crossing the street by the time I left the hotel. I ran hard after him. He turned, tried to aim and fire off a shot, but was able to do neither. Distracted, he almost ran himself into a post, but dodged it at the last moment and entered a dark alley.

I went after him at full speed, too wrought up to consider that I was chasing an armed man and had no weapon myself. Ahead in the darkness, his pistol barked, and I heard the bullet sing into the sky.

I became aware that a third figure had joined the race. I saw my prey pass through a shaft of moonlight, visible for that moment, and then a second man did the same, having come in from a different angle. It was a policeman, a pistol in hand.

At this point I was third in this race. But I was grateful for the intervention of the policeman, and pleased that he had been able to make enough sense of all this to realize who was running the race of the wicked and who was righteous. He might as easily have assumed I was the villain here. Perhaps it was the fact I had no weapon and the other man did that gave him the decisive clue.

I soon lost track of which part of town we were in. I was conscious of shacks and sheds spread across a hillside, then a district of what I first thought were barns but then realized were warehouses, lined up side by side.

One of them had an open door. By moonlight I watched the pursued man enter, followed by the policeman. I entered right behind them, my heart by now about to pound right out of my chest.

The darkness inside was almost like that of a cavern. I halted, then moved quickly to one side so that I was not limned against the doorway. I heard no running feet . . . had they already moved out the other side of the building? I couldn't see how; there was no open door other than the one by which we'd entered.

I stood unmoving, sucking in air, hoping I did not breathe so loudly that my location could be pinpointed by sound alone. When I was able, I held my breath suddenly, and listened.

Somewhere out there in the dark, someone else breathed loudly . . . then I heard an

Irish-sounding voice. The policeman: "Freeze where you are! Hands up!"

For all I knew, he was talking to me. I almost raised my hands, but there was a sudden shot in the darkness. Light flashed; I saw the crouched form of the ruddy-faced man, pistol extended. Then a yell of pain from the policeman, almost simultaneous. Total darkness again. Hammering footfalls . . . a figure racing past me, out the door.

I wanted to pursue him, but I could not. The policeman was groaning pitifully on the warehouse floor. I followed the sound and reached him.

"Help me," he said. "I'm shot."

"Can you get up?" I asked. I reached down, touched him, felt hot blood running fast.

"No," he said. "No." His voice was weak.

"I have to go find help," I said. "Just hang on, hang on. I'll be back with help."

I ran out the door, knowing that the policeman's life probably depended upon my next actions. Unfamiliar with Leadville's physicians and medical facilities, I headed for the police station. Coming out the door was a uniformed officer.

"Sir!" I called. "There's another officer . . . shot. Shot bad. Help me find him a doctor!"

By the light of lanterns the doctor worked feverishly on the injured policeman, and though I prayed he would succeed, the evidence indicated he would not. The policeman's pallor, the glaze of his eyes, the feebleness of his breath, all indicated that the shot had been lethal.

I had been instructed to stay close by, because there were naturally many questions that needed to be asked of me. It was clear that in the confusion of the moment I was being considered a suspect in this incident. It would not be the first time that the perpetrator of a shooting had panicked and gone to fetch help for the very person he'd shot.

I could not linger. Katrina was left alone at the hotel, and the ruddy-faced man was still out there. Quietly I slipped back into the darkness and left the warehouse.

There had been a stray pair of trousers around the jailhouse, some abandoned possession of a former prisoner, and these had been tossed to me as we made our way to find the doctor. Thus, when I entered the hotel again, I at least did so without the indignity of being clad only in long underwear, as I had been when I left the hotel.

The gunshots and activity had stirred the place to life; someone had even gone and fetched the owner of the hotel. He stood in the midst of the lobby. One glance revealed that he had dressed hurriedly after being roused from bed at his nearby house. His vest buttons were through the wrong holes, his collar was undone, and the tail of his shirt hung out on one side. His hair, uncombed, was going up on all directions.

"You there!" he said when I entered. "Are you the one in the midst of all the altercation?"

"Out of my way," I said, shoving him aside and heading up the stairs.

"You! Come back here!"

Ignoring him, I ran down the hall to Katrina's room.

Empty. She was gone. I felt my stomach rise to the vicinity of my throat.

To my room next. She was not in there, either.

I ran to the top of the stairs. "Did anyone see what happened to the woman in room 204?"

"*I'm* asking the questions here, you!" the hotel owner said. "What's this business of gunshots fired in my own hotel?"

A man in a nightshirt and robe stepped

forward. "Mr. Wells, I believe?"

I looked at him, wondering if I knew him. His face was familiar, but I couldn't place him until I noticed the girl who stood beside him, also in a robe. It was Virginia, the talkative young girl I'd met on the stagecoach coming into Leadville. The man was her father, Ezra Birmingham.

"Do you recall me, Mr. Wells?"

"I do, sir."

"My daughter and I moved into the hotel yesterday — a problem with a claim jumper forced us out of the house we'd occupied, and —"

"Please, sir, quickly!"

"Yes . . . I saw the young woman leaving, in a hurry."

"Alone?"

"Yes. She looked frightened. I asked her if she was well. She said she had to get away before 'he' came back. Perhaps she was referring to you."

"No. No, to a yellow-haired man, ruddy features. Tall. A man who has been following her and plaguing her for some time."

"I'd seen that woman before," another man said. "She's nothing but a whore."

I walked down the stairs to him, drew back my fist, and knocked him down with a blow to the chin. He crabbed away, got up, and headed out the door, mumbling something about finding a policeman.

The owner of the hotel blanched, blubbered, and also went out the door. Let them look for the law. They'd find the local police already occupied, and with one of their own officers shot, they'd have little concern about some problem in a hotel.

"Did you see which direction she fled, Mr. Birmingham?"

"No, sir, I did not."

"She went to the left when she went out the door," Virginia said.

"Thank you, Virginia," I said. "I've got to find her."

I ran up to my room, dressed quickly, and armed myself with my pistol and rifle. I left the hotel, turned left, and began searching for Katrina. I searched all night. No luck. No policemen accosted me, and in fact the night passed without any incident at all other than my being approached by two footpads, one with a knife, the other a pistol. I leveled my rifle at them and encouraged them very clearly to move on. They did.

Hard as I searched, I found no Katrina. No trace of her, nor the man who pursued her. Despair mounted. He had gotten her; I was sure of it.

Sometime in the night my hand found a

paper in my pocket. I pulled it out, realized it was the document I'd taken for McCade to sign, giving him the right to pick up his brother's "key" from the police. I wadded it and tossed it away in scorn. It seemed unimportant now, all that nonsense about treasure and secrets and guides to pirate wealth written in the gibberish language of two twin brothers.

Right now all concerns seemed trivial, except finding Katrina and saving her, for there was something in the manner of the man I'd fought that spoke of the most extreme desperation and bad intent. He'd kill her, no question about it. If he'd found her, he probably already had.

I decided it was probably good that she had fled, though. Her instinct had been prudent. He'd known where she was and it would be easy for him to come back to get her. By hiding she was perhaps saving her own life.

But she was also making it hard for me to learn her fate. As I roamed the dark streets of Leadville, I began to realize that I was not going to find her. Not tonight.

As dawn neared I gave up and slowly trudged toward the police station. I saw Marshal Duggan on the porch. Not his normal hours, but then, it wasn't a normal situation for an officer to be gunned down. He watched me approach.

"Mr. Wells," he said.

"Did he live, Marshal?"

"I regret to say he did not. He was a good man, a fine officer. I've just had the terrible experience of telling his wife and little daughter that their father will never come home again."

I stared away, looking at nothing.

Duggan studied me. "What is it about you, Mr. Wells, that seems to embroil you in so much trouble? I can't recall when Leadville has had a visitor who has found so many problems as you have, and in so short a time."

"I don't know, Marshal. I wish I did know. Sir, do you need to talk to me?"

"I do. You were the only witness to the shooting other than the shooter himself."

"The man who shot your officer is still out there. The woman he has been pursuing is gone. I'm told she fled on her own, but I fear that he might have found her. If so, I'm afraid she might be dead."

"Come inside. Let's talk."

I nodded and went in, giving him my weapons. I noticed as he put them safely into a corner of his office that the cabinet that held McCade's key was standing open.

251

The lock was broken and the piece of pipe was gone.

"McCade took his piece of pipe?" I asked him.

"Somebody did," Duggan said. "I found the cabinet that way when I came in. Someone has sneaked in here and taken that piece of pipe. I suppose it was McCade."

"Good for him," I said. "He's got his precious 'key.' "

"Why do you call it that?"

"Long story."

"Why did he want such a foolish thing as a piece of crimped-up pipe?"

"He believes it can lead him to a hidden treasure."

Duggan shook his head and sighed.

"Sounds foolish, doesn't it?" I said.

"Trifling nonsense."

"Will you bring him in for breaking the cabinet?"

"I can fix the cabinet. I just hope he leaves town."

So did I. As intrigued as I'd been by him only hours earlier, he now seemed a trivial, petty figure, obsessed with his own desire for treasure. He was a man who had been willing to live in estrangement from his own brother, trying to reunite with him only when that would bring him a selfish good.

Devil take him. Maybe my book was just fine as it was. My imaginary version of Mc-Cade was perhaps superior to the real one.

All that mattered now was finding Katrina, if it wasn't too late.

Duggan took out a pad and pencil. "Now," he said. "Tell me all that happened."

20

I reached the hotel in a state of near exhaustion. To my pleasure, my room had not been closed off and my possessions removed, as I had feared. I entered and cast myself down on the bed, resting a few minutes but not letting myself sleep. I would not sleep until I had found her, or until I literally could not go forward another step.

But because I was so drained I did sleep, despite trying not to. I slept about an hour, until dreams awakened me. I heard Katrina screaming, wailing. Sitting up abruptly, I stared at the ceiling a moment. The next sound I heard was no fantasy, but a real voice, at my door. A feminine voice.

"Katrina?"

I leaped up, ran to the door, threw it open.

Margaret Rains looked at me through bleary, reddened eyes. She staggered backward, reeking of whiskey. "Well, Mr. Wells!" she slurred out. "I was looking for Katrina!"

"Katrina isn't here," I said. "Katrina may not even be alive."

"What?"

"Step in here. I'll tell you what happened."

"Why, Mr. Wells . . . what do you have in mind?"

I had no patience for a coy drunk just now. Reaching out, I grabbed her arm, pulled her in the room, and slammed the door. I shoved her over to the bed and made her sit down.

"Have you seen Katrina since last night?" I asked.

"No."

"You saw her yesterday morning, though."

"No . . . no."

"Don't lie to me. I saw you slipping around the building. I saw Katrina in the lobby, and then she sneaked upstairs and pretended she'd been asleep, and denied to me she'd so much as seen you. I put up with that lie, but I'll put up with no lies now. You and Katrina have had a scheme of some sort, and maybe something you know can help me find her now."

"Where is she? What happened last night?"

"A man with blond hair and a red face broke into her room. He and I fought, and there was a chase. He ended up killing a policeman before he got away."

"But . . . where is Katrina?"

"That's the question. She left here, fearing he'd come back and find her. Now I'm afraid he *did* find her, and has taken her off and done her harm."

The woman was so drunk that she seemed unable to grasp all this at the speed I gave it to her. "Maybe she'll come back. I hope so. I want to talk to her."

"What kind of scheme have you two had together?"

She chuckled, literally wobbling where she sat on the edge of the bed. "Money, my dear sir. Money. Mu-uh-ney!"

"I suspect I know where you intended to get it. She'd get money from me, you'd get it from Josephus McCade."

"I'll get money wherever I can, Mr. Wells! Hah!"

"You make a poor old drifter fall in love with you, just in case he really does have a treasure. Is that the idea?"

"Not bad, eh? And it worked. It *worked*!" She reached into the bosom of her dress and removed something that she waved before me. "See this? It's the key! It's the key to all the gold a woman could spend in three lifetimes!"

It was the key. The piece of pipe that had

been taken from the cabinet in the police station.

"So it was *you*," I said. "You broke into the cabinet."

She smiled at me. "Daring, eh? Right in the office of the town marshal!"

"I don't care about your key or Josephus's treasure. I want to find Katrina. If she's your friend, you'll help me."

"Mr. Wells, if the man you described has got her, then there's no help left. He swore to kill her. He'll do it."

"Who is he?"

"Charlie. Charlie Luter. Her husband!"

"Husband?" My knees went weak.

"Yes . . . oh! Oh, my! I shouldn't be telling *you* that! That kind of ruins the chances of it all working out, doesn't it!" She laughed. "I guess I'm just too drunk to think straight! But I have so much to celebrate!"

She shook the stub of pipe.

"So you're going to be rich with Josephus McCade, and you're just so happy about it that you don't give a damn what happens to Katrina. Is that it?"

"How can I not be happy? I'm going to be rich! I've always wanted to be rich."

"Congratulations. Now tell me how long Katrina has been married."

"Oh, I don't know. Two years. Maybe

three years. But she left him long ago. Became an actress."

"More than that."

"Isn't that what we all do, Mr. Wells? We offer whatever we have to offer and take whatever anyone will give us for it."

"I'm not interested in your philosophy. I want to know where Luter would take her."

"I can't possibly know. He'd take her out of town, and then he'd shoot her. Poor Katrina! I always was afraid it would come to this!"

"In the letter you sent me, you sounded like you were truly her friend. I now see that wasn't true."

"I am her friend. I was . . . but these things happen, Mr. Wells. Some of us have bad fortune, like Katrina . . . others of us get rich!" She paused and smiled at me . . . an ugly, wicked smile, it struck me. "You're much more handsome than Joe McCade . . . why don't we let him get his treasure, and then you and me can . . . deal with him. He needn't always be around, you know. And then, he wouldn't need his treasure, would he!"

I felt sickened. Exhausted, furious, worried about Katrina, I went to her, snatched the stubby pipe from her hand, and took it to the window.

"No!" she screamed when she realized what I was about to do.

I raised the window, which was already broken by the earlier stray bullet, and heaved the pipe as hard and far as I could. I happened to see it land atop the slightly sloped roof of the building across the street, and lodge there, clearly visible.

With an agonized cry, Margaret ran to the window and began scanning the street below for the pipe. Clearly she hadn't seen it land on the roof. I wasn't inclined to tell her about it.

She turned and slapped at me. I ducked it, and the follow-up slap as well. Then came the cursing. Saliva flying, face distorted, tears flowing, she called me every kind of name conceived by the foulest of human minds.

"Is there anything you can tell me that will help me find Katrina?" I asked when she finally ran out of wind and cusswords.

"No!" she screamed in my face.

"Are you willing to help me look for her?" I asked.

"Hell, no!" she shouted.

"Then get out of here. Get out of my sight. And don't come back unless you decide it's time to become a human being again and care about someone who was your friend."

"You took the key! You threw it away!"

"Go out and look for it, then. I don't have so strong an arm it could have gone very far."

She cursed me again and left. Gone with her was any vestige of the somewhat positive impression I'd had of her upon first encountering her that day in the alleyway when I trounced Slick Davy.

Funny thing. I'd privately laughed at the notion that the female members of the traveling troupe were actresses. Just prostitutes, pretending to be actresses, that's all I'd seen them as. I was wrong. Margaret had been quite an actress indeed. I'd thought she had truly cared about Katrina and had been truly worried about her welfare. Her letter to me had been a masterpiece.

It was all false. Maybe Katrina herself had sat beside Margaret while she wrote it, suggesting words, phrases. She was an actress, too. She'd pretended that the man after her was some obsessed stranger. Dear Lord, he was her *husband*!

But it didn't matter. She was Kathleen's sister. I had to find her, if it wasn't too late.

I looked out the window and watched Margaret emerge from below and begin searching wildly all around the street, the boardwalk on the other side of the street, even under the boardwalk. Someone came by and spoke to her; I watched her turn on them, her face ugly and red, her words vulgar and so loud I could hear them all the way up in my window.

I gathered my baggage and checked out of the hotel, paying for the broken window and other damage from the violence that had occurred. I walked to another hotel, the nearest I could find, and checked into a room.

As quickly as I could dump my baggage, I locked the door and set out again to look for Katrina Ashe, Katrina Luter . . . whoever she was. Kathleen's sister. That was the part that mattered. Kathleen's sister.

I searched for hours, in town, out of town, mostly just riding or walking, looking around randomly.

It soon became clear that one man's eyes could not see enough places to hope to find the missing Katrina. And at that point I stopped looking for her, and began looking for certain others.

I found Baudy digging a grave, and told him who I sought, describing Katrina, describing Luter. I found Hinds sitting on a boardwalk in the shade, whittling and watching the world pass. He was the one I was gladdest to find, because he knew the underbelly of Leadville and those who crawled about on it. The reward I offered was generous, and the collection of it simple: provide me information that would lead to Katrina's rescue, and the money would be paid.

Then I began seeking Katrina again, just in case I chanced to run across her, and went three times past the Swayze House in case she came back there looking for me. That possibility had been the only source of hesitation for me in changing hotels, the chance that she might return to the place she thought I'd be.

But that place was marked. Luter had already tracked her down there, and she could not safely be in the Swayze House again. He'd seek her there.

All this assumed that she was still alive and free of him, and that was a big assumption.

The first times I went past the Swayze, Margaret was still in the vicinity, seeking the piece of pipe. She cursed at me, and the second time threw a clot of dried horse manure my way. It missed.

The day moved on; I did not pause, did

not even eat. At last hunger and fatigue began to overcome me. I stopped by a bakery and bought a loaf of bread, and returned to my room. I ate the bread and drank water, then decided to retire . . . but not before one more search along the street for Katrina.

I didn't see Katrina, but I did see a policeman hauling a kicking and squalling Josephus McCade away toward the jail. A second policeman followed, but was not part of the arrest, merely an observer and apparent enjoyer of it.

I went to that officer. "What's he under arrest for?"

"He beat on one of our local Cyprians who he says lost a key of his that would open up a treasure box . . . something like that. Funny thing is, she whipped him worse than he whipped her. Pitiful little fellow. Crazy, I think."

I nodded. *Should have looked on the roof, Margaret.*

"So the woman will be all right?" I asked.

"She's fine. Soiled doves have hard shells, like a turtle. She's already left town, I believe."

So much for happy endings for money-seeking Margaret. Her key to wealth was gone, as was her relationship to Josephus

McCade. Looks like she'd have to make her money from now on the way she always had.

Just now I felt no sympathy for her or Josephus. They both seemed ugly and small. The sister of the woman I had planned to marry was in danger. Maybe dead. What did their petty concerns or situations matter?

I knew as I made that last search that my motivation had moved beyond the fact that Katrina was Kathleen's sister. My feelings for her had turned into something I hadn't expected, and hadn't wanted.

My last search was no more fruitful than any of the earlier ones. When my last strength was gone, I returned to my new hotel and collapsed into my bed, sleeping like a stone, despite loud and continuous music, laughter, and loud talk from the saloon on one side and the dance hall on the other.

21

When I answered the knock on my door the next morning, Hinds was there, an earnest expression on his face.

"I know where she is," he said before I could even croak out a hello.

I rubbed my face and the back of my neck. "What?"

"I know where she is, Jed Wells. She's alive. She was, anyway, yesterday evening."

My mind woke up and I comprehended. "Where is she?"

"You . . . uh, got that money we talked about?"

"The money comes when I find out for sure you really know something."

"A little bit now, though. Good faith."

I gave him ten dollars. He smiled and nodded and put it in his pocket.

"It wasn't me who saw her. Man named Jack Rumson, who mines up just north of town. Me and him drink together sometimes

265

when he's in Leadville."

"What did he see?"

"There's an old abandoned mine near him. Played out. A house and a couple of sheds. He saw a yellow-haired man and a woman there. He said the man appeared to be treating the woman a little hard."

"When did you learn this?"

"Yesterday, late evening."

"Why did you wait until now to come tell me?"

"I didn't. I knocked on this door until I scarred my knuckles. You didn't answer."

I could have sworn at myself a lot more fiercely than Margaret had. But it wouldn't matter.

"Hinds, why would a man take a woman out to a place like that? Wouldn't he take her farther? Wouldn't he go as far as he could with her so nobody could track them down easily?"

"He would unless he planned to do what my grandpap did when he found out his wife was about to have a baby that was sired by one of his slaves."

"What was that?"

"He shot her dead, then reloaded his pistol and put it into his mouth. Bang."

And as he said it, the prospect seemed so likely that it approached certainty.

"Can you take me there?"

Hinds nodded. "I can show you the way. But I'm not a fighter. That's all I'll do, just show you where it is."

"That's all I ask."

"Are you taking the law?"

I hadn't even thought about that. Perhaps I should.

"I wouldn't take the law," he went on. "You take the law and there'll be a gang of lawmen coming up, and he'll kill her and kill himself right then and there."

"There's no time for law," I said. "We have to go now. It may be too late already."

"You got a horse?"

"I do."

"I ain't got one."

"Can you ride?"

"Yes."

"I'll rent you one. Saddle and all. You have to promise me you'll turn it back in."

"I will. I'll show you the way, I'll collect my money, and I'll ride back."

"It may not be them," I said. "It matches their descriptions. But it may not be them."

"If it is, you pay me."

"You split it with the man who saw them."

"No. You pay me, and you pay him. Same amount."

I'd actually liked Hinds, in a way. Now he

seemed as small and sniveling as anyone else.

"Fine. I'll pay you both. But let's hurry."

As we rode out of town there was a moment of doubt about the wisdom of what I was doing. Maybe I should go to the local law. Not Duggan, but the county sheriff. But that would involve delay, and it had taken long enough simply to rent a horse for Hinds, who proved barely able to ride despite what he'd said.

We headed out of town, Hinds leading the way, going slower than I wished. "Come on, Estepp . . . faster!" I urged. "We have to get there as fast as we can."

"You got the money on you to pay me?" he asked.

"I've got it."

"All right, then."

We headed on.

I didn't keep track of distance, or time, and both passed more quickly than I would have expected. At last Hinds halted his horse, with some difficulty, and managed to turn it and face me.

"The price has gone up," he said. "I think I want both rewards, just for me."

"I wouldn't have thought this of you, Estepp."

"I never claimed to be no holy saint."

"That doesn't make it all right to be a scoundrel."

"You want to know where she is, you give me the money now."

The money didn't much matter. I had enough of it. What galled me was that this man was toying with the safety of a woman I cared about, all for the sake of filling his own pockets.

But I had no choice. I pulled out the money and threw it on the ground. "There it is. Now tell me!"

He smiled, dismounted, and began picking up the cash. Only when he had it all in hand, clutched tightly like a child clutches its toy, did he look at me and grin triumphantly.

"Up that trail, over yonder hill. You'll see a wagon road beyond. Follow it. Not too far, or they'll see you."

He mounted his horse and headed back toward Leadville.

I'd be buying that horse, I figured. He'd have it sold, along with the saddle and other gear, before I made it back to town.

It was a sorry world, filled with sorry people. If I took time to dwell on it, I would have felt thoroughly disgusted. As it was, I was glad just to have him gone.

■ ■ ■ ■

When Hinds was out of sight, I took from its case the rifle that I'd carried through the war, and from the side pocket of that case the long scope that mounted atop it. I'd made a vow years ago never again to use that scope — to keep it always, as a reminder of that vow, but never to use it. I'd broken that vow once, using it to aim a well-placed shot that saved the life of a man being wrongly hanged in Kansas. Today, if need be, I would break it again in a much more significant way. I hoped I didn't have to . . . but I was willing, for Katrina.

Hinds had not lied to me. I found the terrain to be just what he had said it would. I followed the wagon road until instinct told me to stop. Dismounting, I tied my horse and proceeded on foot. Near the top of a rise I moved into the brush and proceeded slowly.

I saw the house and knew at once it was occupied. A curl of smoke came out of the chimney, and I found this comforting. If he'd killed her, he'd not have lingered around . . . would he? If he'd killed her and then himself, it probably had been done the day before, and any fire would have burned out already.

So they were still there. If it was them.

What to do now? I could hardly just walk up to the door and knock.

So I waited. Rifle ready, scope mounted. I waited, and it was the strangest of feelings. I'd done this a hundred times during the war. Waiting, ready to kill when the opportunity came. I'd vowed not to do it again.

Yet here I was.

An hour passed. The smoke from the chimney lessened, then heightened again. Someone had restoked the fire. So they were in there.

Clouds had begun to move in, thick and heavy. Rain was on its way.

There was one window facing me, one shutter open, the other closed. From the distance I was at it was hard to see. I resisted the impulse to sight through my scope. For a while, anyway. When I saw a shadow pass the window, I lifted the rifle and lined the scope up to my eye.

It was Katrina. Alive, moving freely. Thank God.

She moved away from the window. For a long time there was nothing but smoke rising from the chimney.

I almost fell asleep. Tense as I was, I

271

almost dozed. That too had happened to me many times during the war. How could a man be ready to take a life, yet almost fall asleep?

Escape. That was why. I remembered how it had been when I was a boy. Something bad would happen, something jolting, and I would go to bed early, just to escape. Sleep was a salve.

I didn't fall asleep this day, however, just as I never had while perched at some rifleman's vantage point during the war. Always I stayed awake, and did what had to be done.

I prayed that I wouldn't have to do that today.

The clouds were thick now, thunder rumbling. Rain was minutes away at best.

A voice. Male. Muffled by distance and the walls of the cabin. Shouting and angry.

It had to be him.

I heard her shout back. It was hard to hear her clearly, but I thought there was fear in her voice. I almost rose and advanced.

The door opened and Katrina ran out, heading right for me. Her face was white with terror. Behind her, Luter emerged, pistol in hand.

I raised the rifle, sighted through the scope . . . but Katrina was in the way.

She fell, hard. I had him in my sights. I saw his livid face clearly, could remove him with a gentle squeeze of the trigger.

But I couldn't do it. My heart hammered, my breath came as hard as Josephus McCade's had when he and I had talked that last time on the street with Marshal Duggan. And it was as if my finger was made of immobile stone.

She tried to rise but he kicked her down. He cursed loudly.

He lifted the pistol and aimed it at her.

"No!" I yelled, standing.

He gasped, eyes widening, and stepped back so fast he almost fell. He gaped at me, standing there at the edge of the woods, my rifle raised and aimed at him.

"Drop it!" I shouted.

He seemed frozen. The pistol remained in his hand.

"I'll kill you!" I yelled.

Katrina, on her belly, was looking at me with her head uplifted. I'd never seen a face so full of terror.

Luter roared, bearlike, and fired a shot at me. Still I did not fire back. A second shot almost hit me. I shouted one more warning nonetheless.

Please God, don't make me have to kill him. I didn't want ever to have to do this again.

He aimed the pistol this time at the back of Katrina's head.

If I had been frozen until now, I was no longer. At that point my skill, my training, my experience, all came together and I did what I had to do.

My finger squeezed down and Luter fell, a bullet passing through his head, creating a red spray and bringing death in a span shorter than an instant.

He collapsed. The sound of my shot echoed out across the landscape. I heard a birdcall, and the rustling of windblown leaves.

Then Katrina's sob. She rose, crying hard, and ran toward me. I laid down my rifle and took her into my arms.

It began to rain.

There were things that I later would realize I should have done very differently after my rescue of Katrina. I should have reported the entire event to the law, gone through the interviews and statements and court hearings. But I did not. Katrina and I laid the body of Luter inside the cabin and burned the cabin down. She said she could not bear the thought of talking of her ordeal to the law or the court, and I, in the weakness inspired by a growing love, did it the way she wanted.

We did return to Leadville, however, though Katrina hid in an empty barn outside of town while I quietly went on into the city limits. I returned my horse and in its place bought two others. Two saddles as well.

The rain grew terribly hard. I waited it out in the horse dealer's barn until it lessened. Then I rode out on one horse, leading the other behind.

My route took me past the Swayze. On the ground, lying in a glistening puddle, I saw the little stub of pipe that I'd tossed in anger out the hotel window and onto the roof. The rain had washed it off.

I dismounted and picked it up. Should I try to get this to McCade somehow?

No. I wanted only to get out of Leadville as fast as I could. Given what had happened out north of town, I did not want to visit with the local law just now.

There was always the mail. I could send the "key" to McCade in care of the Leadville police.

Leadville had one last surprise for me as I rode out of town for what I assumed would be the final time. I looked to my right, just a random glance, and in an alleyway I saw Yates McCade, simply standing there, staring at me.

I rode by, not stopping, but a block later I did. *Perhaps I should go back and confront him, or report his presence to the police.*

But they already knew Yates was still on the loose. And McCade knew it too, yet still lingered in Leadville despite the danger.

I rode on, finding Katrina safe at the place I'd left her.

"Where do you want to go?" I asked her.

"Anywhere. Just away from here."

"Denver?" It was a purely random choice.

"I've been to Denver," she said. "I liked it."

"Denver it is, then," I said.

We rode.

22

John Battle, editor and friend, sat across the table from me, watching me sip whiskey from a dirty shot glass. Lying before him was a copy of *Harper's Weekly,* open to an inside page nicely illustrated with an engraving of author Jedediah Wells. The single greatest piece of publicity I had ever received, based upon an extensive and honest interview I'd given a month before . . . yet John Battle was not happy about it. So unhappy was he, in fact, that he'd traveled all the way to my rented dive in Denver to tell me in person that he was unhappy about it. And, I suspected, to attempt a rescue of what he rightly perceived as a crumbling human being.

"Come on, John," I said. "Give me my due. My name is now known by far more people than before. Few authors receive that sort of attention from such a major publication."

"Yes . . . and few authors would use the occasion of that attention to make themselves appear to be a half-crazed, drunken dissipate, either."

"It's not that bad. I simply let him see me as I am." I lifted the glass and took a sip.

John Battle sighed. "You didn't drink before. Not in this way, anyway."

"I hadn't been abandoned by a woman I love at that time. I had no cause to drink. Now I do."

There was worry in his expression. "How long has she been gone?"

"Katrina Ashe walked out of my life exactly one month and a half after I brought her to Denver."

"Her rooms were next door?"

"That is correct. I'm not an immoral man, even if she was, at times, an immoral woman."

"Jed, pardon me for saying this, but from all you've told me about her, it might be for the best that she left you. I mean, the woman was conducting a trade in prostitution right in the very rooms rented for her by a man in love with her and who had rescued her from a dangerous situation."

I stared at my glass, thinking that John didn't really know the half of it. I'd told him much, but not the true facts of Luter's death. I'd presented it that Luter, who I didn't identify by name, had committed suicide, and that the sheriff's department in Lake County, Colorado, had done a thorough investigation.

None of that was in the *Harper's* story, nor any mention at all of Katrina Ashe or my Leadville experience. I'd been half-drunk when I gave the interview, and had inflicted a lot of damage on myself and my public image . . . but I'd not been so drunk as to tell *that* story.

"Katrina was not, is not, a good woman," I said. "She's far from what her late sister was. But I'd come to love her."

"I think what you'd come to love, Jed, was who Katrina reminded you of, not Katrina herself. How could you love her? You rescued her from danger, took her out of a miserable and wicked life, rented her rooms, set up a bank account for her, bought her clothing and furniture and tried to help her find a legitimate way to support herself. And I swear, I believe that in time you would have married her —"

"I would have."

"— yet she repaid you by going back into prostitution right under your nose, betraying you, and in the end, abandoning you."

I poured myself another drink.

"Put the whiskey away, Jed. It's not like you to do this."

I took another sip. "No, I suppose it's not. But I just don't feel like me anymore."

He stood, sighing, and walked about the room a little. I looked at the picture of myself in the copy of *Harper's*. "I look decent enough, anyway."

"Oh, yes. The engraver did a fine job of catching those bags that are beginning to grow under your eyes."

I looked more closely at the picture. "Really?"

"Really. You're changing, Jed. You're killing yourself slowly, all over a woman who isn't worth it, if I can come out and say so."

"Don't insult her," I said. "I've knocked people down for that."

"I doubt you'd succeed with me."

"Probably not." John Battle stood six feet tall and weighed in at well over two hundred pounds and was as manly as his surname. When he wasn't pounding submitted manuscripts into shape, he spent his time pounding a punching bag at a gentleman's club down the street from the publishing house.

"When am I going to get a look at that manuscript?" he asked.

"I don't know, John. I've been thinking of rewriting it completely."

"Can I at least see the first version to see if perhaps it's better than you think?"

"It's not that I don't think it's good," I clarified. "I think it's outstanding, in fact. I let a friend in Memphis read part of it and he was quite impressed."

"If you're sharing it with the world, how about sharing it with your editor, too?"

"The issue is that I had a chance to meet again a man upon whom I based the central character," I said. "And I may meet him again. I hope I do, any day now."

"I know, Jed. Josephus McCade. You told me about meeting him in Leadville, or is your brain so whiskey-pickled you don't remember? You met him and now you think you should redirect your entire story. I might suggest otherwise. You're writing a novel, not a biography. The fictional man need not be a mirror of the real one, and I might argue, *should not* be a mirror of the real one. I'm not looking for a lawsuit of some sort here. Wait, what was that you said about meeting McCade again, any day now?"

"Let me show you something," I said. I rose and went to a desk. From it I produced a piece of sawed-open pipe, and from inside it plucked a small, folded piece of paper. I handed it to John Battle.

"Take a look at that," I said.

He unfolded it, squinted at it. "This is gibberish. Not to mention terrible penmanship."

"I shouldn't have opened that thing up, John, but for the last four months I've done all sorts of things I shouldn't have done. That 'gibberish' is supposedly a key to a great pirate treasure hidden somewhere along the coast of North Carolina."

He looked at it some more. "Yeah, no doubt that's the case."

"It's half a key, anyway. The other half is lodged inside the mind of Josephus McCade.

"It's not even real words."

"It's a secret language. Have you heard of siblings coming up with their own languages when they are small? Usually twins do it, I think. That's a sample of one right there."

"This is a language?"

"Of sorts. Josephus and Spencer McCade came up with it when they were children. They taught it to their uncle, apparently a simple but good man who spent his time poking around in caves and so on along the Carolina coast, where there were indeed pirates in years past. He's the one who is said to have found a treasure of pirate gold. He wrote down directions as to where to find it, and gave half to Josephus, half to Spencer. Trying to force them to reconcile with one another after they had a falling out. I suppose he thought a good case of gold fever might cure all else that ailed them."

"How did you wind up with it?"

"It's too long a story for me to want to tell right now. But the truth is, I shouldn't have that. It should be in the hands of Josephus McCade. I've lately begun to feel guilty for having something that is rightly his. So, I've written him a letter, in care of the Leadville police, telling him where I am and inviting him to wire me to make arrangements to obtain that little piece of paper you hold in your hand."

"I simply cannot believe this is a true key to treasure."

"Whether it is or not, Josephus believes it is."

"How do you know he's still at Leadville? He may not even get your letter."

"I know. I've worried about that. If I don't get a wire from him soon, I may have to go back there myself and see if he's still there. If he's gone on, I'll have to see if I can find out where he went."

"Jed, you spend your life roaming around doing things you think are your duties to other people. All these Andersonville folks, and now this old drunkard."

"He also falls into the category of Andersonville folks. And don't disparage drunkards. I've come to have a whole new perspective on drunkards lately."

"So what's the point of all this?"

"The point is, I still think the real Josephus McCade beats my fictional version all hollow, and I'd like to talk to the man some more and see if I can't make my book all the better for it."

I took another drink. He watched me.

"Jed, what's this drinking all about? Truthfully. I don't think it's really about the woman. Not entirely. Tell me if I'm wrong."

I waited a long time before I quietly answered, "You're not wrong."

"So why are you trying to destroy yourself?"

Another pause. "Have you ever vowed to do something . . . or to never again do something . . . and then broken that vow?"

"Everybody's done that."

"Is that right? Well, I'm no exception."

He studied me. "Jed, is this something going back to the war? To your sharpshooting days?"

"In a way." I looked at him, but what I was seeing was the red spray that had erupted from the head of Luter when I eliminated his life to save Katrina's. For the sake of that woman, who had since abandoned me, I had broken a vow I had made to God himself, never again to take a life with that rifle and scope. Done that for her . . . and now she was gone. No wonder I drank. "In a way," I said again.

"Whatever it is, Jed, you've got to get past it. Pull yourself together. I'll not watch a good author, not to mention a person I happen to think highly of, destroy himself over things that can't be changed."

"That's the thing," I said. "That's the rub. Why is it there is so much in life that can't be changed? Why does it have to be that way, John?"

"I'm an editor, not a philosopher. Not a clergyman."

"I'm not sure what I am at all."

"You're an excellent writer, Jed. You've got treasures of your own to share with the world. I'd like to see you get back to doing it."

I stood and walked to the window, where I looked out across the Denver landscape. "I'm putting the whiskey aside, John. I'd decided it even before you got here. After today, no more."

"How about, after that last drink I just

took, no more? How about that instead?"

I nodded. "All right."

"I am sorry she left you, Jed. And I'm sorry about whatever else it is that plagues you. I wish I could change those things. But I can't."

"I appreciate the thought, anyway."

"Jed, let me take the manuscript. Let me see what you've already written, and maybe we'll find that it's much better than you thought."

I nodded. "Very well. But I may yet have to change it."

"McCade is probably gone from Leadville, Jed. If he'd been there he'd have responded right away, as eager as he'd be to get his hands on this piece of paper. By the way, is this the only copy of this thing?"

"I made another copy, just in case something happened. I don't understand it, of course. But it's the same thing that's written there, as closely as I can duplicate it."

"Go fetch me that manuscript, Jed. I want it in hand before you go changing your mind on me again."

"All right."

I went to my room and pulled the stack of papers from a drawer. Without even glancing at them, I took them to John Battle and placed them in his hands.

"Very good," he said. "I already like it. I like the way it feels in my hand. I like the heft of it."

"You're a fine editor, if you can evaluate a book without even reading it."

"Aren't I, though!" He grinned. "You do mean what you said about the whiskey, don't you?"

I went to the table and picked up the bottle, still half-full. While John watched, I took it to the window, which I opened. I thrust the bottle out and turned it upside down, and watched the whiskey drain onto the ground.

"Very good, Jed."

"It's easy to grow fond of that liquid fire."

"Jed, you need to get away from this place. You've grown stagnant here. You came here with a woman who was bad for you, and now you're left alone. Put this place behind you."

"I think I will."

"Visit Chicago. Louisville. New York. Boston. Atlanta. Anywhere."

"How about Leadville, Colorado?"

"To find McCade?"

"To begin looking, anyway."

"Let it go, Jed. There's surely no treasure."

"Maybe not. But after a dozen years of living on a river island looking for his lost key, digging up the corpse of his own brother, being tracked by a bloodthirsty cousin, he has a right to see for himself, I guess."

"I suppose. At least it will get you out of these rooms. Do me a favor, Jed: forget about Katrina. Forget about Kathleen. One is gone and the other is dead. Move on with your life and start being a writer again. A sober one. One who gives interviews that show him as the kind of person he *really* is."

I nodded. "Let me know what you think of the book."

"You can count on it."

23

Leadville, Colorado, on a rainy night. I'd left this town on a dismal, rainy day, and returned to it on another. I was different . . . thinner, bearded now. And alone. The town had changed, too. New buildings where empty lots had been, and a few empty lots where buildings had been. Including the Swayze House. The hotel that had survived a fire while I was in Leadville before hadn't survived a second one. The charred lumber was gone, but the foundation remained. A sign declared that a new Swayze House would soon arise where the old one had been.

I pulled my collar high and rode slowly down the muddy street, watching water stream from the front of my hat before my face. A new hotel had opened at the far end of the street, and I rode there and checked in. Anonymity appealed, so I borrowed John Battle's name and put it on the ledger.

I stabled my horse, put the saddle in storage. I'd traveled light; the clothing and goods I'd brought filled only part of the wardrobe.

I walked to the restaurant where I'd purchased my first meal in Leadville, and bought a steak. I'd sworn off whiskey, but the steak demanded a beer. I ate slowly, looking out through the window into the dark and wet night, and wondering where Katrina was now.

Had I ever really loved her? Or was my editor right, and my affection for her had been only a ghost of the love I'd once had for Kathleen? Did it matter now? She was gone. I would not have her, nor would I have her if I could. There could be no happiness with a woman such as Katrina. Nothing that would last.

When I was finished, the rain had lessened. I walked out onto the empty, glistening street, and made my way to the police station.

Even that had changed. Work had been done inside, things moved around. Duggan's office, though, was in the same place, just with a new door. But he was not there.

I recognized the policeman on duty, but he did not remember me. I greeted him and told him I was looking for an old friend I thought might be in town. His name was Josephus McCade.

The name brought a reaction. The policeman cocked up one brow. "What are you? Some kind of journalist?"

"No. Why do you ask that?"

"Then you're a relative?"

"I'm not."

"In that case, I'm not inclined to answer your question."

"Why not?"

"I'll say no more. But no one who comes looking for Mr. Josephus McCade is going to find out a single thing about him unless I know exactly why he wants to know."

"I've got something that belongs to him," I said.

"Leave it with me, then."

"This I'd like to give him myself."

The policeman stood and leaned toward me. There was nothing but dead seriousness in his face. "You listen to me, sir: I don't know who you are or exactly what you're after, but I'm tired of strangers coming into this town trying to find Mr. Josephus McCade on this pretext or that. If you think you could build a reputation by doing that man harm, you'd better know that you'd have the entire city of Leadville crawling down your neck. Josephus McCade is a treasure of this city, and we stand for no one trying to harm him."

"Why would I harm Josephus McCade? I just want to return an item to him that he'll be glad to get. And since when did he become a treasure of the city?"

"You going to be around town a day or so?"

"I could be."

"Then you be on the street tomorrow at noon. That street right out there. You'll see how this city feels about Josephus McCade, and why."

I returned to my room, wondering what dream I was moving in. Could this be the Leadville I'd known? Could the Josephus McCade just spoken of so protectively be the one of my experience? How many Josephus McCades could there be?

I retired that night wondering what the devil was going on in this town.

There was a new store building on Chestnut Street. A gleaming painted sign declared its name: BIRMINGHAM DRY GOODS.

Behind the counter, Ezra Birmingham beamed healthily from behind a crisp white apron, his beefy arms bound by black armbands. I watched him through the window and inwardly wished him the best.

Clearly he'd decided against mining and had taken to a more familiar road of commerce.

I saw little Virginia come skipping up the aisle and out the door. She turned and smiled up at me, looking quizzical and friendly all at the same time.

"I know you, mister," she said. "But I don't know where from."

"My name is John Battle," I said, wondering if she would figure out the truth on her own.

"I'm Virginia. This is my father's store."

"It's a fine one."

"He's going to get rich here. I'm glad he decided not to be a miner. He wouldn't be a good miner. But he's good at running a store."

"Well, that's good to hear. I wish him the best."

"When will the parade start?"

"Is that what's happening here?"

"Sure! It's the parade for Josephus McCade, exterminator of footpads!"

"What?"

She grinned at me from the side of her mouth. "Didn't my father and me ride on a stagecoach with you one time, mister?"

Just then I heard the thrumming of a bass drum down the street, followed by a hideous, atonal blare of bugles. Virginia leaped up and down. "The parade's starting!" she said.

People lined the street on both sides. Half of them at least seemed to have simply materialized from nowhere; I couldn't guess where they'd come from. The music from down the street grew louder, then the processional came into view.

At the lead was Duggan, riding a big white horse, and behind him the assembled uniformed policemen of Leadville, other than those busy maintaining order on the street sides. Behind them were some other men with plain clothes but badges on their chests. County officers, I thought. Then another man preceded by a sign declaring him to be a visiting federal marshal. Then assorted town leader types, and a gaggle of merchants.

A gang of assorted locals blowing bugles followed the merchants, making a racket that at rare moments seemed to approximate a melody of sorts.

"Is this all about Josephus McCade?" I asked Virginia.

"I *do* know you!" she said. "You're the man on the stagecoach who writes books! But you look different."

"I've lost some weight and grown whiskers. Is this all about Josephus McCade?"

"Look!" she declared, pointing. "There he is!"

Indeed, there he was, borne in a chair that had been fitted with long rails on either side, like something Far Eastern royalty might ride around upon. I gaped to see Josephus McCade himself, cleaned up and shiny as a new apple, bouncing along five feet above the ground, waving with one hand while clinging to his bouncing chair with the other. The men carrying him wore grins, dark suits, and cloth vests over their coats that declared them to be some sort of federation of local merchants.

Behind them were boys, carrying signs that extolled the virtue and valor of Josephus McCade. BANE TO THE LAWLESS! One of them read. MCCADE THE BLACKLEG BLASTER! read another. HERO! HERO! HERO! another banner proclaimed. And LEADVILLE DISDAINS VILLAINS. Another one: LOT JUMPERS BEWARE!!!

Then, most bizarre of all in my estimation, another group of like-dressed men ended it all up, carrying a coffin that had no doubt been built for the occasion by Harvey Soams, undertaker and maker of final abodes for the eternally unmoving. On the side of the coffin was the word BLACK-

LEG. The gang of pallbearers all looked very happy and at times would reach up and slap the side of the coffin, as if slapping at its absent but symbolically present occupant.

Virginia, like most of the crowd, cheered and clapped as the little parade passed.

"Virgina, you're right: I am Jed Wells, the man you met on the stage," I said. "Could you tell me what is going on here?"

"Why did you lie about who you were?" she asked.

"Oh, I knew I'd changed a lot and I wanted to see how much. I wondered if you'd recognize me. Should have known I couldn't fool Virginia Birmingham."

She beamed. "Should have known! I ain't nobody's fool!"

"This parade . . ."

"Have you not heard what Josephus Mc-Cade did, Mr. Wells?"

"I just got back into town. Long absence."

"Looks to me like you spent some of that long absence tilting the bottle. I can tell from looking closely at the little veins at the end of your nose."

Oh, Lord, was it that obvious? A little girl could look at me and see the signs of dissipation? I hadn't poured out the whiskey a moment too soon.

"About Josephus . . ."

"He saved a senator's life, and killed a footpad with his own bare hands."

"Josephus did that?"

"Yes, and now he's the hero of the whole county. The whole state!"

"I'll be! When did this happen?"

"A month ago. They should have had this parade a lot sooner, but nobody thought of it until the merchants had a meeting last week."

"How did Josephus save a senator?"

"Senator Aaron Cornfelt was in town. I don't know why. His wife got sick up in her hotel room and he left the room late at night to go looking for a doctor. In Leadville you should never leave your room late at night, not unless you want trouble. That's what my father says."

"What happened?"

"A footpad of the worst ilk attacked him with impudent viciousness, trying to free him of his coin purse."

I had the distinct impression I'd just heard a bit of a local newspaper account quoted back to me.

"And . . ."

". . . Out of the darkness the hero came, bearing in hand a broken bottle wielded like the sword of Arthur or the sling of David, and with it attacked the heartless blackleg in a manner his villainous self was most suited to comprehend."

"You memorized the whole story?"

"I'm good at memorizing. I memorize a lot of things. Want to hear the Constitution?"

"Later."

"I can do it in pig Latin. I can do anything in pig Latin. 'Omeo-ray, Omeo-ray, erfore-whay art-ray ou-thay Omeo-ray!' "

"Impressive."

"Why do they call it pig Latin? Pigs don't talk that way. Pigs don't talk at all."

"Tell me about Josephus killing the footpad."

"He drove the piercing shards of the broken and glassine weapon into the flesh of the neck of the brute, opening a crimson fountain that gushed forth death for the blackleg while giving life to the noble Senator Cornfelt, friend of the laboring Coloradan."

"So Josephus is a hero."

"Yes. And he's a great artist as well. The newspaper gave him money to draw a picture of himself rescuing the senator. It's on display over in the public meeting hall."

Amazing. I watched Josephus as he was carried on down the street, still grinning and waving. He turned a corner and went out of sight, and most of the crowd surged off the boardwalks and followed after him.

"Did you know he had been nothing but a sad old drunkard, half-crazed by the bottled demon, but he proved himself of finer mettle than he appeared?"

"Is that what the paper said?"

"Yes."

"I knew he was crazy. I knew he drank."

"Is your book printed yet? The one I did the title for?"

"Not yet. It'll be a spell before that happens. Tell me something else, Virginia: has Josephus McCade been around town for a long time now? Or has he come and gone?"

"Then newspaper said he has gone back and forth between Gambletown and Leadville, pursued by a relentless one-armed human demon. He's also been seen often over in front of where the Swayze House used to stand, searching and searching and searching, and talking about a treasure that he nearly had, but somehow lost."

It was getting harder to tell where the extemporaneous narrative left off and the lurid newspaper quotations began.

"He is a tragic but heroic figure," she said.

"You have a dramatic way of talking."

"I told you: I like to memorize things."

Her father's voice boomed from inside the

store. "Virginia!"

"Got to go," she said. "I'll see you later, Mr. Wells."

If ever I had a daughter, I'd want her to be like this bright and chattering child.

I found the meeting hall and studied the large drawing Josephus had done. It was almost funny, in its way, with its depiction of a barrel-chested, handsome, towering Josephus lunging toward what looked like a human being halfway through transformation into a devil. To the side was, presumably, the senator, his hands over his face as he gaped in amazed appreciation at the salvation just given him by Josephus.

There was something familiar in the look of the man Josephus was shown attacking. His build was broad and bearish, and he had an oddly straight, dark arm. Like it was made of wood.

24

Marshal Duggan looked at me with a frown as I entered his office, then stood and put forth his hand, his face changing a bit as he recognized me. It wasn't fully an expression of happiness to see me, but he was friendly enough.

"Mr. Wells! So you've come back to join us! You haven't returned to Leadville to generate more adventures and problems for me, like last time, have you? I have plenty of them here without outside help."

"I have not, sir. I've come back to return an item to someone who lost it."

"Ah, I see. You look different, sir."

"I've grown some whiskers. Lost a bit of girth and pounds. You recognized me more quickly than most, though."

"Why should you lose weight? You were not a heavy man to begin with. Have you been well?"

"My health is fine, thank you."

He gestured toward the cabinet. "We never found who broke in and took that piece of pipe. You remember that pipe, don't you?"

"Yes, I do. I know who stole it, as well."

"Who?"

"Her name was Margaret Rains. She was one of the members of that traveling troupe of actors."

"Ah, yes! That bunch! I remember them well. I assumed at first it was Josephus McCade who broke into that cabinet, but I later learned I was wrong."

"Is Margaret Rains still in town? Do you know who I mean?"

"Very pretty lady, if I recall. Lord, what a gaggle that troupe was . . . they came to a bad end, you know."

"How so?"

"The man running that little show apparently had fallen in love with one of the women in it. She disappeared, and he grieved so much he started taking it out on some of the others. Finally this Negro fellow with them, the one who wore a towel on his head and went by some kind of fancy name, decided things had gone far enough. He put a pitchfork through his boss and took off west. Ain't been caught that I've heard."

"Lord Clancy."

"That's right, that's right. Lord Clancy. The district attorney says his name was Clancy Jefferson, really, or something close. He tried to find out more about him, but there was little to be found except some minor criminal record."

"So the troupe is no more?"

"Nope. All gone. Scattered to the four corners of the world. Good riddance."

I felt rather numb at this grim news. Katrina Ashe left ruin in her wake, everywhere she went. She'd left me on the road to being a wasted drunkard. Apparently she'd left her earlier cohorts in even worse condition.

"I'd ask you where you've been, Mr. Wells, but I already know."

"You're a reader of *Harper's*?"

"That's right. I've got my copy at home. Read it and said, 'I know that man. That man was in Leadville.' And now here you are again. What can I do for you?"

"I came in hopes of finding Josephus Mc-Cade. I thought it might be hard to do, but the town obliged me by parading him before my eyes."

"Unlikely hero, that man. But he did a good thing. You know our one-armed friend, the one who beat Slick Davy into jelly?"

"McCade killed him?"

"Jabbed him in the neck with a bottle. The fellow staggered off bleeding. He'd taken a room in the Swayze House, probably paid for with stolen money. He managed to knock over a lamp and catch the place afire. All got out but him. He was burned to a crust. I'm the one who actually found his body, what there was of it."

So much for Yates. Josephus McCade could afford to be paraded down the street now. No one to hide from.

"You've answered my question then, Marshal. I wanted to be sure that was really who McCade attacked."

"You want to see McCade himself?"

"Yes."

"He's got a house now. Courtesy of the good senator whose life he saved. He saved the senator's missus, too, in one way of looking at it. She was a very sick woman and probably would have died if her husband hadn't gotten the doctor to her . . . which would not have happened if he'd been killed or rendered senseless by a footpad."

"I guess Josephus is a happy man. And lucky in his way."

"He is. Who wouldn't be happy, having a whole town make so over you? And rumor has it the senator plans to get some sort of resolution issued, thanking McCade for what he did."

"Wonders never cease."

"We almost lost our hero in that cell yonder one evening. Probably about the time you vanished from our town. We hauled him in one night for having beaten up on the very Margaret Rains you already mentioned. He claimed she lost the 'key' to some treasure. Loco talk. But we put him in that cell, and he nigh choked to death. The man couldn't breathe. I actually took him some whiskey to open him up. It worked well enough to keep him from dying in there, but that was about all. I let the poor devil out early because I didn't want a man smothering to death in his own cell, right in the open air."

I remembered Josephus's gasping and wheezing in the presence of things that panicked him.

"Marshal, there's something I have to admit about that situation. It wasn't her fault that it was lost. It was my doing."

"Your doing?"

I told him about flinging the pipe and its contents across the street and onto that roof, and of recovering it later when rain washed it down.

"I shouldn't have left Margaret Rains in a situation to get her hurt. It was my bad judgment . . . but at that particular time bad judgment was something I was adept at. I've come back to try to make amends to him. I want to give him back his lost 'key.' "

"He'll appreciate that."

"Where will I find him?"

"In his house." He told me how to reach it. "But he's probably not there. Today he'll be out celebrating himself along with the rest of the town."

"Why such a fuss? Not to minimize the importance of saving a senator's life or anything."

"The town has seen a steady rise in its rough element," said the marshal. "We work hard against it, but it happens all the same. What McCade did had a symbolic impact. He was the one man in this town who did what everyone else wished they had the courage to do. I figure this may herald an arising of vigilantes . . . not always a bad thing, even if I do say so wearing the badge of official law on my shirt."

"I'm not trying to spit in the silver chalice here, Marshal, but Josephus well may have been seizing an opportunity to help himself instead of doing it out of his love for American politicians. The one-armed man had pursued him a long time, with very bad intent. He was McCade's own cousin, you know."

"I didn't know."

"Yates McCade. Murderer of his own father, according to Josephus."

"Well, I'll be hanged!"

"He'd have murdered Josephus, too, once he got him to translate something for him."

"What was inside that pipe, Mr. Wells?"

"This." I showed him the paper. "It's written in a language only one living man in this world knows, and that's Josephus. He and his brother made up that language when they were just little boys. Put what's on that paper together with what's in Josephus's head, and you supposedly have a wealth in pirate gold waiting for you on the coast of North Carolina."

"Could there really be something to it?"

"There could be. Or it could be pure fiction."

"I wouldn't mind finding a trunk full of gold."

"Who would?" I took back the paper and put it in my pocket. "Thank you, Marshal. And sorry about all the times before, when I seemed to always be in the midst of whatever trouble came up."

"This time we'll have a quieter stay in

Leadville, won't we? Tell me we will."

"You have my word on it. No trouble at all."

Based on the description and directions given by Duggan, it was easy to find Mc-Cade's new home. Though no bigger than a shack, it was stoutly made of good yellow lumber and looked sturdy and pleasant. Much newer and nicer than the place Mc-Cade had lived in on his island near Memphis.

McCade was not home. I settled down in the yard, leaning back against a tree, and waited. I had bought a loaf of bread from that same baker I'd visited during my first Leadville sojourn, and sat back with the bread on my lap. I pinched off pieces and ate them, then began sharing with a hungry-looking stray pup that came wandering up.

By the time McCade came staggering home, having enjoyed a midday celebration in one of the local saloons, I'd surrendered the loaf to the dog, pulled my hat down over my eyes, and dozed off. I awakened to find McCade right in front of me, looking down at this intruder in his yard.

It took him a couple of moments to realize who I was.

"I'll be!" he said. "Jedediah Wells. Looking a little different, but still Jed Wells, I do believe."

"Hello, McCade. Congratulations on your new status as Leadville hero. Quite a job you did."

"I think I'm going to be famous. There was a man in town from *Frank Leslie's Illustrated* two days ago. He talked to me the longest time and wrote down notes. Another man drew pictures."

"I was in *Harper's Weekly* myself lately."

"I know. Marshal Duggan showed it to me."

"You no longer have that fear of lawmen like you used to?"

"Not like I did. Not since I turned hero. The policemen like me now."

"Quite a parade today."

"Thank you. Why are you back in Leadville? You vanished the first time."

"I came back to bring you this." I reached in my pocket, pulled out the paper that once had been inside the pipe, and handed it to him.

He looked at it, eyes widening as he realized what it was. His hand trembled as he read the words. And abruptly, he burst into tears and sobbed aloud.

"Josephus? What's wrong?"

"The key," he said. "It's the other key."

"That's right. And I owe you an apology. I should have had that to you long ago. And I shouldn't have opened it up."

"Why did you do it?"

"Curiosity. I knew I'd not be able to read it. I just wanted to see what the writing looked like. Josephus, I've been off the right track for quite some time now, but I'm trying to get back onto it. I want to make things right by you. Now you've got both keys. You can go look for your uncle's treasure."

He tilted his head back and laughed, tears still streaming down his face.

"What is it, Josephus?"

"One key, and not the other. Then it all turns around. The other key, and not the one."

"You do have both keys. One in your hand, the other in your head."

"Can I give you some advice, Mr. Jed Wells? Don't ever trust the mind of a drunk to hold anything in memory too long."

"You've forgotten it."

"I've forgotten it. Just little bits and pieces of it is all I can remember. Oh, why did I let myself destroy the written one!"

"Because of Yates."

"Yeah, yeah. Yates. Because of my cousin.

But what did it matter? He couldn't have read it anyway."

"If codes can be broken, then secret languages can be figured out as well. You did the right thing."

"But now I've lost it. It's too late to remember."

"Memory can return, Joe. I'll bet if you study that new one, it will trigger parts of the other one back to your mind again."

He hung his head and let his arms hang limply at his side. The piece of yellowed paper fluttered in his fingertips, blown by the wind.

"Don't despair over this, Josephus. You'll figure it out. It will come back to you."

He shook his head and walked slowly to his dwelling. Opening the door, he vanished inside. The door closed behind him.

I'd figured that my presentation would be the capstone on an excellent day for Josephus McCade. I guess I'd figured wrong.

25

There are times when writing comes hard, and times it requires only a little effort. Then there are those rare moments when the words burst forth like a new spring, as if from some outside source, and it's all one can do to keep the pen moving fast enough to keep up with the flow.

This was one of those times. I don't know what it was in my meeting with Josephus McCade that triggered the flood, but something had. I went to my hotel, had a small table brought up, purchased several writing tablets at a local store and a box of pencils, and sat down and began writing.

I hoped that John Battle was enjoying working on the draft of the novel I'd left with him. Because enjoyment was all he'd get out of it. I knew now that I would discard that draft. It had been only the predecessor of the real story I was supposed to discover, a sort of literary John the

Baptist heralding the approach of the true Messiah, which only just now was emerging.

For almost a week I worked feverishly. Little food, not much sleep, and no liquor at all. Odd, about the liquor. During my days of waste in Denver, liquor had held me in a strong grip. I'd drink it most of the time and think about drinking it when I wasn't. Now I gave it no thought at all. The writing, the story, had taken its place.

Finally, after six days, I was past it. The frantic, driven quality vanished from my work and I wound down, working slower and slower until at last it was time to lay the pencils aside and go back out into the world again.

I did so with several pads full of words stacked on the hotel room table. I had captured the book when it was ready to be captured. From this point on it would be a matter of working and reworking, shaping until it was honed to what it should be.

For two days I relaxed, roaming Leadville and this time venturing out more into the surrounding countryside, exploring the mines, the surrounding communities. I went back to Gambletown, and thought about Katrina. I stood on the spot where we'd stood together, before we mounted my horse and rode out. I wondered where she was now, and what she was doing. Despite myself, I still cared. I wondered also how it could be that two sisters could be so very different. She had reminded me so much of Kathleen, but at the points that mattered most, she differed from Kathleen as a demon differs from an angel.

I had not seen Josephus McCade since our meeting in the yard of his little house. And, perhaps oddly, I'd thought little about him, only about the fictionalized version of him at the center of my novel.

Late afternoon. I had returned to my hotel after a long hike outside of town, where I'd let my muscles stretch and work and enjoyed the warmth of the sun on my back. What had looked like recreation had actually been work; I'd spent my walk reflecting on what I'd written, thinking of a few key points that could stand some revision.

My mind was still distracted by such thoughts when I approached my hotel room door. I had almost reached my hand to the knob before I realized the door wasn't completely shut. And it had been shut when I left.

I put my hand beneath the light jacket I wore, and touched the butt of my pistol.

When I went in, Josephus McCade was there, face dark and grim, eyes hollow, mouth hanging open. He reeked of liquor.

My writing pads were all over the place, pages torn out and ripped, thrown everywhere.

"Who the hell do you think you are?" he demanded of me. "You think you can write about any man you please, say all kinds of lies and rubbish? You can't do that, Jed Wells. You can't write about me."

Looking at my ruined work, I could hardly draw a breath. This all seemed inconceivable, a nightmare in progress. God, let me wake up. I could never re-create that book, not in the way I had during that long burst of inspiration.

"Josephus, what have you done?" I grabbed up some of the ripped sheets. Surely I'd be able to piece them back together, enough of them to save the book, anyway.

He came to his feet and pointed a wavering finger at me. "It's you . . . you're like a curse to me! It all would have been fine if not for you showing up!"

"What are you talking about?" I picked up more sheets and started to sort them. He roared and reached for another pad, and I lunged toward him. "Don't touch it!" I yelled, and he was wise enough to obey.

"It's your doing," he said. "It was you who stole the key from the undertaker's cabinet. If you'd just stayed out of my life, I'd have found it there myself. It was you who had the key when Margaret lost it . . . your fault, not hers, but I was so fierce angry with her that I beat her! I lost her because of that! I got throwed in jail because of that, and nigh died, nigh smothered! And I was without Spencer's key for so long because you had it! You! You had no right to it, but you had it! And during that time, I ceased to remember the words of my own key!"

He waved his hand around the room. "All this paper, covered up with your sorry scribbling . . . you come to my house, you'll see paper everywhere, too. Me trying to remember what the key said. I ain't remembered yet! Because of you!"

"You get out of this room," I said. "You have no right to come in here and destroy my work!"

He waved his hands and gave out a scream of the purest frustration I'd ever seen a man display. "You take away my chance to finally get the treasure I was meant to have . . . you take my key and keep it for months, me thinking it was lost forever . . . and now you steal my life and my story and turn it into something that'll give you a treasure of your own, and me having nothing — nothing! — to show! It's wrong, Jed Wells! It's wrong as hell, and I ought to kill you for it!"

Angry as I was, and reluctant as I was to admit any such thing, I could actually see what he meant. From his point of view I'd been no more than a thief. As much a thief as Slick Davy, or Yates. My actions had cost him any chance at the fortune he'd longed for since even before the war . . . and now I was indeed, in effect, taking his life story and turning it into something that would generate for me a great profit.

His next words, however, made no sense to me. "And now, now, you come back into town and hand me the key when it's no good to me no more . . . and you bring back the dead. Bring back the very dead!"

"What are you talking about? What 'dead'?"

"Yates. Yates ain't dead. I killed him, but he ain't dead. I saw him. I swear I did. You came back to Leadville, and he came back too. Damn you! Damn you for it!"

He pushed past me, kicking torn pads and papers all around, and stormed out the door.

He truly was insane. Those moments of lucidity often disguised it, but times like this made it clear. Josephus McCade lived much of his life in a world generated by his own mind.

At that point I became sure there was no treasure and never had been a treasure. There might not even be an Uncle Clooner. Maybe not even a real secret language. Just gibberish scrawled on paper. All these things might be entities just as false and fantastic as dead footpads who inexplicably come back to life.

I began picking up papers, straightening them, putting together shredded pieces. As I worked I began to find hope. The work was torn up, but not gone. With time I could reassemble it and have it recopied. As soon as I got the fragments together and in order, I would take them to the local bank and have them put in the vault, in case Josephus ever felt inspired to attempt another vandalism like this.

The next afternoon I stood at the cemetery gate, talking to Baudy Wash and feeling a little bit foolish for it. I'd tried to frame my question in a sensible way, but it still sounded for all the world as if I were asking about the possibility of a dead man coming back to life.

"I just want to be sure that the man who

died when the Swayze House went up in flames really is who they said he is," I explained. "Was it for certain the one-armed footpad who Josephus McCade had stabbed?"

"That's who they say it was, sir."

"You saw the body?"

"What was left of it . . . you couldn't tell much about him, sir."

"One armed?"

"Yes . . . no. Really he had no arms nor legs either one. They was all burned away, sir. Ghastly sight. Awful smell, too. Have you ever smelt a burned-up man, sir?"

"Once, during the war. So it could be at least possible that the man they found in the hotel wasn't Yates . . . the one-armed man."

"I guess so, sir, but who else would it be? The fire started in his room, and that's where they found him. Well, that's where they calculated he must have been. Though with the way that building pitched and fell, seems to me he could have fell in from some other part of the building."

"He'd been stabbed in the neck. Could you see the wound?"

"No, sir. The flesh was too burned away for that."

"So really, it could have been someone

else in the hotel."

"They accounted for all the folks on the ledger, sir."

"But it could have been somebody else anyway. Someone who didn't sign the ledger. Someone who was visiting the hotel."

"Maybe you ought to ask the marshal, sir. All I know is that I seen what looked like a big piece of coal, laid in a coffin, and they told me it was a one-armed footpad who'd tried to rob a senator, and had gotten stabbed and then burned up."

"Thank you, Baudy. Maybe I will talk to the marshal."

"Why you asking this, sir?"

"Because a man told me that he's seen the man who is supposedly in that grave. Seen him in the last day or two, alive and well."

Baudy lifted his brows and looked quite nervous.

"Don't worry. It was probably a mistake."

"Who seen him, sir?"

"Josephus McCade."

"The same one who stabbed him!"

"That's right."

"Seems to me he would know that man pretty well."

"It does. Which is why I've swallowed my pride enough to come ask you these questions. It doesn't make a man look very smart to go around asking if anyone has seen a dead man up and walking around."

"Sir, in the kind of work I do here, I don't question nothing that nobody asks. I've seen too many things I can't figure out."

"You're a true believer in ghosts and such, I take it."

"Yes, sir. I only know what I've seen, sir."

"Good day, Baudy."

"Good day, sir."

Duggan, sitting at his desk and probably wondering why this bothersome author just kept coming around, scratched his chin and looked at me in a way that told me he was quite uncertain about what I had asked him.

"I've not been asked a question like that before, I must say. But yes, I feel reasonably sure that the man we buried was this Yates."

"Reasonably sure . . . but not absolutely."

"Not absolutely. The damage to the body was extensive."

"So if there had been someone else in the room at the time of the fire, and if Yates went in and was noticed, and out again without being noticed, it could be that the presumption of his death is incorrect."

"That's possible. It seems unlikely, though."

"But it would explain why McCade seemed so sure that Yates has, in his way of looking at it, come back from the dead."

"Isn't it more likely that the man is simply insane? Anyone who could actually go around feeling angry because he believes someone has come to visit town and caused a dead man to get up again is not a sane or normal man by any accounting of mine."

"I agree with you. As he was saying those things, and tearing up my work besides, I agreed strongly with that very sentiment. But there's something about McCade . . . there's always that initial certainty that he's simply loco, talking nonsense . . . but then things come along to suddenly make it seem like it could be true. The treasure, for instance. The whole business seemed completely implausible, until Josephus told me how it came about. And it all fit. There really were pirates along the Carolina coast. If there really was an uncle, and he really did poke around in the caverns and coves, he could have found such a thing. And there really could be a language the boys developed together . . . I've heard of that before."

"Or, it could all be nonsense."

"I know. I know. I can't decide. One moment I'm sure of one thing, the next moment another thing."

"My advice is to forget about it entirely," Duggan said.

"I feel a certain responsibility, though. Because of me, he lost an opportunity to have both parts of his key together. If there is a treasure, it's now out of his reach, because of me."

"There's no treasure. He's just a crazy, dreaming man. Now, do you want to bring any charges against him related to the damage to your book?"

"No. I was able to piece it back together. It's now locked in the bank vault."

"A good move. Now, again, I suggest you forget about Josephus McCade. He's fine, better off than he's ever been. This town has declared him a hero, he has a house given to him free and clear, and the danged United States Senate is probably going to issue him a medal or something. He's got his treasure as far as I'm concerned."

"You're probably right."

"I am. Now, if you don't mind, I've got some work to do."

26

I wasn't sure what had caused me to awaken. My hotel, sandwiched as it was between two businesses perpetually generating noise, had helped me revitalize a skill that I'd lost to a degree once I escaped Andersonville: ignoring extraneous sound.

There was the usual muffled cacophony coming at me from both sides, but in the midst of it something that stood out: a clanging bell.

The Leadville fire bell. I'd heard it that night in the Swayze. Something somewhere was burning.

I stood, sniffing the air. No smell of smoke. At least this time it wasn't the hotel I was in that was burning. I went to the window and looked out. People were running toward the northwest. Craning my neck, I made out a flickering light in that direction. When I raised the window and stuck my head out, I realized the fire was in the general vicinity of Josephus McCade's dwelling.

Actually, it seemed to me the fire might actually *be* at Josephus McCade's dwelling.

My first thought was of lot jumpers. But that seemed unlikely; they tended to do their diabolical thievery on lots just being occupied. McCade's dwelling wasn't brand-new enough to be a likely target for lot jumpers.

An accident, then. Or arson? Somebody jealous of McCade's newfound status? Or angry over the death of the man he'd killed . . . whether that was Yates or someone else?

It probably wasn't McCade's place at all — I couldn't tell for sure from where I was — but the possibility was enough to make me dress and head onto the street. Because of the late hour, a dangerous time to be out in crime-rich Leadville, I strapped on my pistol and hid it beneath a light but somewhat long jacket, which I buttoned at the top but left hanging open below.

I'd not gone far before I realized it really was McCade's dwelling that was on fire. Firefighters were busy controlling it, keeping nearby structures dampened down and the flames as contained as possible, but clearly the house itself was already hopelessly gutted.

My angle of approach brought me to the rear of the little building. Most of the flames were toward the front of the structure.

A man was already there, watching. "Did McCade get out?" I asked him.

The man turned and looked at me. It was Soams, the undertaker. I realized I was close to his building, something I had not noticed the first time I saw McCade's house.

"Hello, Mr. Soams," I said.

He looked at me in a most unpleasant fashion.

"Did he get out?" I asked again.

"Yes, he did," Soams replied. "He must have been drunk, though. He had to be dragged out of the place."

"You saw it?"

"Yes. And the man who dragged him out is, as far as I'm concerned, much more a true hero than this McCade ever will be. It's remarkable to see a man, so drunk he cannot stand, being pulled from a burning building by a man with only one arm."

I gaped at Soams. "Dear Lord," I said. "Oh no. How long ago, Soams?"

"I don't know. Fifteen minutes. Twenty."

Leaving Soams where he was, I ran around the burning house, looking for a policeman. There were three right at hand.

"Pardon me," I said to them. "There's something you should know. I believe this fire was set deliberately, and the man who set it is a one-armed man named Yates."

The officers looked at one another in amusement. "Is that right?"

"Look, I know it sounds insane, but —"

"Insane is right," said another officer. "Yates is the name of the footpad McCade killed."

"Well, he didn't really kill him, to be exact about it," the third officer said. "The man did get away and into his hotel room."

"Yes, where he died of his wounds and knocked his lamp over in the process."

"In any case," said the first policeman, "there is certainly no way that you saw Yates dragging McCade out of that house tonight. Yates was burned to nearly nothing when the Swayze House went up."

"I don't think that was really Yates," I said. "McCade himself told me that he's seen Yates since then."

"Well, he's seeing a ghost, then."

"McCade was insane, mister. He may have been the hero of the moment, but he was as loco as a weed-eating cow."

"Why do you say 'was'? Is he dead?"

"I think he is. I think he's inside there." He waved toward the house.

"Aren't you going to try to get him out?"

"Friend, have you gotten close to that place? Can you feel the heat? Too late is too late. He's burned up."

They were right. If McCade was inside, he was already gone. But if Soams had seen what he believed he'd seen, McCade wasn't burned up at all. And neither was Yates.

I returned to Soams, having to circle farther around the house this time because the flames were higher and the heat more intense. "Which way did they go?"

"Why should I be standing here talking to you? You broke into my business. You threatened to get me in trouble with the police. You — eeep!"

I had him by the throat, gripping it tightly in my left hand. My right drew out my pistol. "Tell me . . . now."

"They . . . they were going . . ." He lost his ability to speak and simply pointed.

"On horseback?"

He tried to talk. I let up on his throat a little. "On foot."

"What's up that way?"

"Mines . . . a lot of mines. Several abandoned."

"A place a man could torture another without being heard?"

"Torture?"

328

"Yes, torture. I have reason to believe that the one-armed man might torture McCade to get certain information out of him. Unfortunately it's information McCade no longer remembers."

"You'll never find them. There are so many mines and shafts and shaft houses. They could be anywhere, if they are there at all."

"If they can be found, I'll find them."

But I wasn't nearly as sure as I had sounded. I moved through the darkness, winding my way between shaft houses and storage sheds and little miner's huts, all made of rough lumber. Other than what intermittent moonlight came, this was a very dark area.

For twenty minutes I searched, occasionally glancing back toward town to see the progress of the fire, which was now at its most spectacular level.

I stopped, trying to think this through logically. The prevalent belief was that Yates was dead. But it was based on little evidence, simply a burned body and the presumption that Yates had remained in the hotel room after he entered it. I hadn't seen the burned corpse, but I knew enough of fire to realize it could devastate a body to the point that it was impossible to discern identity, even sex.

Based on what Soams had seen, either Yates indeed was alive, or Josephus McCade had the odd distinction of being pursued by not one, but two, one-armed men. Not very likely.

So Yates was alive. And after Josephus's keys. One of them, the written one I'd given to him, Josephus could provide. The other one, memorized and then forgotten, he could not. Therein lay the danger. Yates would take a long time to be persuaded that Josephus truly did not possess the information.

I remembered what it had been like to see Yates moving toward me in that cellar, ready to be rid of me because of what I had seen.

Poor Josephus. I had to find him.

I wondered why Yates was not wearing his wooden arm. Maybe he'd lost it; maybe he only wore it part of the time. Good thing for me he had not worn it tonight, for whatever reason. It had made him more readily identifiable.

I searched ten more minutes, then decided I had best return to town and try again to persuade the police to believe me.

How could I do that? I wasn't even sure I believed me.

At that moment I heard a yell. A man crying out, voice muffled, in either great fear or pain. It came from behind me, up a rise, from somewhere amid a jumble of crude buildings.

I drew my pistol and advanced. Another cry . . . it was Josephus.

I almost yelled to alert them to my presence, then restrained myself. Yates might do something drastic if he felt threatened.

Following the direction of the last outcry, I came upon a large, looming building that stood on an odd tilt. I couldn't understand this until a blink of moonlight through a gap in the sailing clouds revealed the remnants of a rockslide around the place. It had been pushed off its foundations and was clearly not a safe building.

I heard another yell. McCade was pleading, clearly in pain. I advanced toward the dark and looming mouth of the damaged door.

From somewhere inside I saw a glow of flickering light. At first I took it for a random reflection of the fire raging in the town below, but a second look verified that it came from within.

I advanced, entering, my pistol out and ready. Another scream, louder this time. I turned a corner and reached the central room of this structure, which apparently was a combination shaft house and mining office headquarters, now abandoned.

The light I'd seen came from two sources: a lantern hanging from a nail on the wall, and a torch in the single hand of Yates. McCade was chained to a support beam, his shirt ripped open. Clearly Yates had prepared this place in advance. Yates moved the torch near his chest, closer, closer, causing McCade to turn his head to avoid the flame, making his skin redden and blister beneath the heat.

"Tell me!" Yates said. "Tell me where it is!"

"He doesn't know, Yates," I said, lifting my pistol.

Yates wheeled, the torch flame flaring and streaking as he did so. "Who the hell . . ."

"Let him go," I commanded. "He doesn't have the information you want. It's too late."

He held up the torch, letting it illuminate my face. "Ah, yes . . . I remember you," he said. "The cellar. You watched me take care of that damned footpad."

"Where's your wooden arm, Yates?" I asked. "Termites? Dry rot?"

"Funny man. Real funny. It's burned up, that's where it is, burned up with that whore woman in the hotel."

"So that was the body they found, was it?

Who was she? Was her name Margaret?"

"Maybe it was."

"They think you're dead, Yates. She was burned up so badly they thought the body was yours. Now, no more talk . . . let Mc-Cade go."

"No. No. Hell, no!"

"You've got a torch, McCade. I've got a pistol. Think about it."

"Think about this," he said.

The torch fell from his hand and rolled across the slanted floor, the flame nearly dousing, then heightening again as the torch came to a stop. In the same moment Yates pulled a small pistol, previously unnoticed by me, from the waistband of his trousers. I raised my pistol to fire, but he was half a moment quicker. The shot was loud in the enclosed, tilted room. My arm burned sharply, then went numb, and the pistol fell from my hand.

I fell back, and that saved me from the second shot. It went past me and out the wall. Yates cursed and prepared to fire again, but McCade put out a foot and managed to kick one ankle out from under Yates, making him stumble and delaying a third shot.

I couldn't find my pistol, and couldn't move my right arm to pick it up if I had found it. And I'd never been able to shoot left-handed and hope to hit even a moun-tainside. So by instinct I went for the fallen torch instead, grabbing it in my left hand and rushing toward Yates with it while he was still off balance.

The flaming end hit him under the chin; flames licked up the side of his face and he let out a howl. To my surprise, something on him lit. As the torch pulled back from him, I saw it was his hair and beard. The man must have used some oily ointment in both, for they flamed up brighter than the torch itself, causing him to scream and flail about, slapping at the wreath of fire circling his head. But the fire only grew hotter.

I tackled him, dropping him to the floor, and to his good fortune found an old piece of tarpaulin lying within reach. I used it to smother out the flames around his face. For a moment he lay still, whimpering and weeping, the tarpaulin across his face and me kneeling beside him . . . then he lunged and pushed me backward. I fell onto my back, landing atop a flat wooden surface, slightly higher than the floor like a very low platform, made into a square and badly rot-ted from water that had come in through a big hole in the roof above. The wood sagged and creaked beneath my weight, then gave way. My body passed through, feet swinging down. I groped for a handhold and managed to brace myself by gripping with my left hand the edge of the flat platform through which I'd fallen. The wood was less rotted there and did not yield.

But the weight of my body strained my fingertips, pulling at them, trying to drag me into whatever abyss was below me. I could give myself no help with my right arm. It was still unmoving and mostly numb, though a dull pain was now beginning to rise in it, and I could feel warm blood coursing down it and dripping off my fingertips. As I watched Yates get up, casting aside the tarpaulin and advancing toward me with his ruined hair and beard still smoking, I comprehended that I'd fallen atop a lid constructed to cover an old mining shaft. It opened straight down below me and I was literally dangling over a pit that was God only knew how deep.

"Help me up, Yates," I said. "I put out your beard and hair . . . now you help me."

"For what?" he said. "So you can tell the police how I beat that footpad to death?"

"They already know that. They figured that out all on their own. Help me, please."

"No. No. You'll just try to get the treasure instead of me. And I'm the only one who is going to wind up with that gold. It was my father who found it. I was the one who should have been given the keys, not him, not his brother." He gestured with contempt at the chained Josephus McCade.

"I don't have the key anymore," McCade said. "I memorized one of the instructions, destroyed it . . . then forgot it. I already told you that, Yates! Nobody knows where the treasure is now."

Yates did not like hearing that. He cursed, grabbed up the torch, and shoved it against McCade's chest. McCade let out a scream. Yates, unrelenting, left the torch burning against him for several seconds before pulling it back.

"Did that help you remember, cousin? Did that stir your mind a bit?"

McCade went limp, groaning.

My fingertips were strained to the point of giving way. My body felt as if it weighed half a ton. I would fall in moments, and the prospect of plunging into that unknown darkness below was as unwelcome as the prospect of dropping into hell itself.

Desperate, I began moving my feet, slowly, looking for some foothold that would help me. And I found one. Almost out of reach, but not quite. I couldn't look, of course, but it felt like a spike of some type, sticking out of the wall. Maybe just a big nail on which a lantern once hung when this was an active mine. Whatever it was, it was strong enough to let me put some of my weight on it, and I pushed up a little, easing the strain on my hand and fingers somewhat. But I remained in a precarious position and would not long be able to stay in this situation.

"God, my face hurts!" Yates said, leaning over, grimacing. "Burns . . . burns . . ."

"Help me, please," I said. With my other foot I was searching for an even better foothold. Surely there had been a ladder of some sort on the side of this shaft. Maybe still was.

If so, I couldn't find it.

"Yates, don't do this," McCade pleaded. "For your father's sake, don't do it!"

"Damn my father! He never cared a thing for me. You and Spencer, that's all that mattered to him. I was nothing to him. He had every notion of leaving me with nothing while you two would end up with a treasure! I despise him more even than I despise you!" With that, he shoved the torch against Josephus again, holding it there even longer this time.

My foot touched something on the shaft wall to my right. It was solid and thick, and felt like the rung of a ladder. I put my weight on it and it held. My pose was still quite awkward — one hand gripping, the other dangling and numb, one foot on a nail or spike on the left side of the narrow shaft and the other on a ladder rung on the right side. But at least I was not in as immediate a danger of plunging. Even so, I was helpless.

"Yates, let me go and I'll try to remember what the key said," Josephus pleaded. "Maybe if I try long enough I can remember. Just don't burn me anymore."

"You remember now. Right now! Or I'll burn this place down around you, like your house down there! How'd you like that, huh? The big-town hero, man with his parades and his new house and everybody praising him because they think he killed a really bad man . . . how'd you like to burn up twisting on a chain, hero? How'd you like that?"

"We can find the treasure together, Yates. I've got one of the keys, and in time I can remember the other parts, I'm sure of it! We'll go to Carolina again and search all along those places that Clooner used to go, and we'll find that treasure. We'll split it even."

"No. No. It's mine. Nobody else's. It was my father who found it! *My* father!"

He shoved the torch against Josephus again.

And suddenly everything changed. Josephus let out a great roar and slammed his body back hard against the beam to which he was chained. The building, already tilting and damaged, groaned. He slammed again and the beam gave way. Josephus fell back atop it and the building shifted, cracked, sagged, but did not immediately fall. Clearly, however, that beam had been a key support for this structure.

The floor moved a little as the building shifted, which caused Yates to fall down and drop the torch again. It rolled like before, but this time went out.

McCade pulled his chain free of the beam, simply slipping it over the bottom of the beam. He picked it up and swung it, gladiator-style, at his cousin as Yates tried to get up again.

The chain caught Yates on the side of the face, driving him down and laying open a wound. The floor shifted again, and suddenly my foot slipped off the spike and my weight pulled in a whole new way, causing my fingers to let go. Yates and McCade and the lantern-lit room above vanished and I was swallowed by blackness.

Somehow, though, I was able to swing my

body toward the ladder on which my other foot still rested. I grabbed it, and so saved myself from falling into the pit. My right arm, however, remained useless to me. I climbed anyway, and used my head to butt up against the base of the broken shaft cover. It was heavy, but I was able to move it. Scooting it inches at a time, I opened an increasingly large space above me.

I could hear the fight continuing, and it sounded as if Josephus had lost the advantage. Yates was cursing, taunting, and from the things he said and the noises McCade was making, I believed he was choking Mc-Cade.

With effort given that I had only one working arm, I managed to climb up out of the shaft and throw myself onto the slanted floor. McCade was on his back, Yates atop him, using McCade's own chain to choke the man.

The building groaned and moved again. I fell over, but got up. Taking the lantern off the wall, I swung it up and brought it down on Yates's back. It shattered, spilling burning fluid down Yates's shoulders and back. He howled, leaped up, flailing about and screeching. I kicked him and he staggered back toward the shaft. Another kick and he fell, plunging in flame down into the hole, and making a terrible thud when he hit bottom.

The building caved in atop me and Josephus McCade.

27

It would take some time for my right arm to function like it used to. The doctor had said as much and I'd gotten used to the idea. But John Battle didn't take the news well. My right hand was my writing hand, and try as I would I couldn't train myself to temporarily use my left one, and I'd never been able to dictate to a transcriptionist and produce anything other than garble. So for the time being I was out of the writing business.

Before long, John Battle made his peace with the situation. He liked the first draft of my book, but as I told him Josephus McCade's true story, he agreed that the book would be better for the reshaping and redirecting I had given it. As soon as my arm was healed, I would go back to work. The future would go on much as the past had.

For Josephus McCade, there would be differences. When the building fell, it crushed his legs. Though the town of Leadville rallied to his aid, and I recruited Monty Wilks to help me bring in some excellent physicians to oversee his case, it appeared that Josephus was destined to be partially crippled the rest of his days.

The legal side of things went more brightly. The Leadville policemen who had refused to believe me when I told them that Josephus McCade had been kidnapped by a man they thought dead apologized to me. The body at the base of the shaft generated an inquiry, but in the end, the entire matter came to nothing. Josephus and I gave our statements about what had occurred. They matched, and the entire matter came to nothing.

The charred body from the hotel fire, the body Baudy Wash had buried under the belief that it was Yates, was exhumed and examined by a leading coroner brought in specially for that purpose, at my expense. Soams was impressed. He'd heard of this fellow, a real celebrity among those who dealt with the dead, and had him autograph a coffin lid for him while he was in town.

The coroner determined that the burned body had indeed been that of a woman. Various circumstantial evidence backed up the theory that it was probably Margaret Rains. Whether she had associated with Yates in the normal course of her life of prostitution, or had learned enough to see him as a possible route to that treasure, we would never know. She went back into the grave, which was left unmarked because there was no way to be fully certain it was Margaret. Baudy put flowers on her grave, saying he thought that even an anonymous whore deserved at least one consideration when she was laid to her rest.

I didn't remain in Leadville long enough to see McCade through his recuperation. I returned to Monty's for a time, enjoying the luxury of his fine home, and when I was able, beginning there the process of rebuilding the final version of *The Lost Man,* a book that would go on to even greater success than had my first novel.

With John Battle's help, I made some arrangements for part of the profit from that book to go to Josephus McCade. I believed he deserved it.

I kept up with Josephus's progress through wires and notes back and forth to Leadville between myself and Duggan, who chose not to run again for office in the next election and was succeeded by a man named Kelly. After that I gradually lost touch with Josephus McCade, though I did receive news that eventually he did begin to walk again, using crutches, and that he'd left Leadville as abruptly and mysteriously as he'd left McCade's Island.

I wondered if maybe he finally had remembered what had been in that original key, memorized and then forgotten.

It would be five years before I found the answer to that question. Really, I never found the answer in a definite way . . . but I liked it that way. It was better to retain just a little bit of question and mystery when it came to Josephus McCade.

I was in Chicago when I spotted the little art studio and saw the sketch in the window. Another view of the *Sultana,* very similar to the one that Josephus had drawn on the wall of the Horsecollar Saloon in Gambletown. The Horsecollar, sorry to say, did not survive because Gambletown itself did not survive. It vanished from the American landscape of living towns like so many other towns of the West, its buildings eventually weathering away. I always planned to go see if Josephus's sketch remained in that old saloon building, and if so, to cut it off the wall and keep it, but like so many of life's intentions, it just never came about.

Back to Chicago. I saw the distinctive sketch in the window of that art studio and went in to find a full display of similar work, all obviously done by Josephus McCade. Now, though, he was using the name of Garner — clearly a borrow from the fictional character he had inspired me to write about. I considered it an honor.

Best of all, though, was one particular sketch, a small one, that was displayed in one dark corner of the studio, almost like an afterthought. It was a dramatic scene of men battling in a tilted, lantern-lit shaft house. The one that obviously was supposed to be me was presented in a particularly dramatic and heroic pose, and I admit I was flattered.

I bought that piece of "Garner" art and carried it out of the studio. I never had it framed, and seldom even went back to look at it, but it remained a treasured possession thereafter.

Did Josephus ever find his treasure? Did he use it to finance a true career in art? A few times I thought about ferreting out the answer, but as I said before, somehow it was best to keep a bit of mystery and question intact when it came to McCade.

But I like to think he did finally remember what his uncle had written in that note that resided so many years in the little piece of pipe Josephus guarded so closely through the war, through Andersonville, and sought for so many years along the banks of the Mississippi. I like to picture him putting the message from the two keys together at last, and moving along the rugged Carolina coast on those crutches of his, until at last he found a particular cavern or grotto, and in it the pirate gold that his uncle had wanted him and his brother to have.

I hope it happened for him. And I hope it was every bit as gratifying as he'd always thought it would be.

ABOUT THE AUTHOR

Tobias Cole is a pseudonym for well-known author of Western fiction. He lives in Tennessee.